# the new rules of HIGH school

# the new rules of
# HIGH
## school

## Blake Nelson

Viking

**VIKING**

Published by Penguin Group

Penguin Young Readers Group, 345 Hudson Street, New York, New York 10014, U.S.A.

Penguin Books Ltd, 80 Strand, London WC2R ORL, England

Penguin Books Australia Ltd, 250 Camberwell Road, Camberwell, Victoria 3124, Australia

Penguin Books Canada Ltd, 10 Alcorn Avenue, Toronto, Ontario, Canada M4V 3B2

Penguin Books (N.Z.) Ltd, 182-190 Wairau Road, Auckland 10, New Zealand

First published in 2003 by Viking, a division of
Penguin Young Readers Group.

10 9 8 7 6 5 4 3 2 1

LIBRARY OF CONGRESS CATALOGING-IN-PUBLICATION DATA

Nelson, Blake, date-

New rules of high school / by Blake Nelson.

p. cm.

Summary: Seventeen-year-old Max Caldwell has been the perfect high school
student—on the honor roll, captain of the debate team, and soon-to-be editor
of the school newspaper—but during his senior year, he begins questioning his
approach to life and things start to change.

ISBN 0-670-03644-7 (hardcover)

[1. High schools—Fiction. 2. Schools—Fiction. 3. Interpersonal relations—Fiction.
4. Newspapers—Fiction. 5. Conduct of life—Fiction. 6. Portland (Or.)—Fiction.]
I. Title.

PZ7.N4328 Ne 2003    [Fic]—dc21    2002153369

Printed in U.S.A.

Set in New Century Schoolbook

Book design by Nancy Brennan

For Frieda

"Youth understands its environment instinctively. . . .
It lives mythically and in depth."

—*Marshall McLuhan*


"You got a problem
Come on over. . . . "

—*Echo and the Bunnymen*

# Part One Spring

*April is the cruelest month*, I thought as I sat with Cindy at the basketball game. It was from a poem we did in AP English. I couldn't remember the rest of it, something about spring and nature and how things die and are reborn. It was one of those poems that didn't really make sense. It was more about the sad sound of the words and the way it moved through your mind like a dream.

Cindy was following the game. She was wearing her blue sweater, which looked good with her blonde hair and blue eyes. She had her feet up on the bleacher bench in front of us. Her chin was resting on her hand. She watched one of our guys steal the ball and run the length of the floor for a layup.

I watched too. Something was off between Cindy and me. We hadn't been talking lately. In fact, we'd *stopped* talking. When she picked me up she hadn't said a word. We didn't talk in the parking lot or coming into the building. Now we sat watching the game. And not talking. It wasn't that we didn't love each other anymore. Maybe we loved each other too much. Maybe our relationship was so secure, we didn't need to talk.

I didn't know. I had been working so hard that year, my junior year, and now it was April. I had made honor roll again. I was captain of the debate team. I was probably going to be a National Merit Scholar. The day before I had been named editor-in-chief of *The Evergreen Owl* for next year.

But with all that going on, something had gone wrong with Cindy. Even though she was the perfect girl. Even though we were the perfect couple.

I watched her. I couldn't remember why we were together.

Evergreen won, 42 to 37. It was a Tuesday night game so there were no parties. I had to go home anyway. I had AP History to study for.

We walked into the parking lot. "Hey Max! Hey Cindy!" someone called out.

"Hey," I called back.

Rain was falling, a light, gentle, April rain. It was springtime. It was the cruelest month.

We ducked our heads and hurried to Cindy's car. It was her parents' red Ford Explorer. I had always thought it was funny: cute little Cindy in that big bulky car.

It didn't seem funny now.

We both got in. She found her key and put it in the ignition.

"Uhm, could we hang out a sec?" I said.

"Why?" said Cindy, looking at me.

"I just . . . do you wanna talk for a minute?"

"Here?" she said.

All around us, people were walking back to their cars, not just students but parents, families. They looked strange in our school parking lot.

"Yeah," I said, drawing a breath.

Cindy looked at me. She looked forward. She let go of the keys and sat back. "Is it something serious?" she said.

"Kind of," I said.

"Okay," she said. She settled herself. She waited for me to speak.

"No, I just . . . I wanted to see how you feel about things."

"About what things?"

"Just like, how things are going with us," I said. "You know . . . are you still happy with everything?"

"What? Aren't you? Do you want to break up?" She was joking.

Then her face changed. "Oh my god," she whispered to herself. "You want to break up." Her body stiffened. She stared into the rain-blurred windshield.

People were still walking by. But fewer people. The parking lot would be empty in ten minutes.

"It just seems like . . . " I said. "Like last weekend at Gabby's. You barely talked to me. And you kept running off with Dominique and those guys. And shaking up beer cans, and spraying people. . . . "

"I wasn't running off. It was a party. They were spraying *us*. What was I supposed to do?"

"It seems like you're getting more popular. You're hanging out with different people. And next year I'll be doing the paper. . . ."

"Max, what are you talking about? I'm not popular. I don't *want* to be friends with Gabby Greenberg."

"It just seems like—"

"And who cares who I'm friends with?"

There was no stopping it now. It was over. I still loved her but it was over. Before, I had thought if I ever broke up with Cindy it would be because I stopped loving her. But I still loved her. And I was breaking up with her anyway. It was just happening. And now that it was started it couldn't be stopped. Because that would hurt her more.

"But they like you," I said. "And next year will be so different. I'll be doing the paper. . . ."

"You want to break up. You do. I can feel it in this car." She sat quietly for a moment. "You've already made up your mind."

I didn't deny it.

"I always wondered what it would be like to break up," she said quietly. "And this is what it's like."

"Doesn't it seem like we're heading in different directions?"

"You're not going to tell me the real reason," she said. "This popularity thing, you're making that up."

"I'm not making it up."

"Is it sex?" she said. She turned toward me. "You know I want to. You were the one who wanted to wait until the prom. If you don't want to wait . . . "

"It's not that."

"What is it? Max, tell me."

I sighed. "I don't know."

Silence filled the car. Raindrops fell gently on the roof.

I wanted to speak. I couldn't. Tears formed in my eyes. "I feel like . . . " my lips began to tremble. "I feel like everything's changing. Don't you see? We don't talk. It feels old. It feels like the best part . . . is over."

"Tara always says you're too serious for me," she said, in a strangely cheerful tone of voice. "I mean, she likes you, but she thinks you worry too much."

"Maybe that's it," I said. I took a long breath. We didn't talk for awhile. She wiped tears off her face.

"What about the prom?" she said, sniffling.

"I don't know."

"Could we still go together?"

"I guess so. People will expect us to."

She thought about it. "No, we can't. If we're not really together."

I nodded my agreement. She sniffled more. Then she started to cry. It was the saddest sound I had ever heard.

Eventually, I had to go. I dabbed my own eyes on my coat sleeve. I found the door handle. I let myself out of the Explorer.

"I'll walk home," I said.

"No, no," she protested. "I'll give you a ride Max. You can't walk home, it's raining."

"No, I'll walk."

7

"Max, please." She cleared the tears from her face. "I'm sorry I'm crying. Let me drive you."

"Really, I want to walk."

She looked at me. She wiped her eyes. "Oh god, Max, I *love* you. . . . "

"I know. I love you too. I wish—" But I couldn't finish it. I shut the door. I started walking. The red Ford Explorer sat there, by itself, in the empty parking lot. It was still there when I turned down Shattuck Road.

# 2 – – – – – – – – – – – – – – –

I walked. It was good that it was raining, and late. The road was quiet. No cars came. I cried and then I wiped my face with my sleeve.

I walked. I thought about my future. Not college or my career but other people I would love. People who would not be Cindy. Grown women whom I would meet years from now, at future jobs, or in distant cities I would live in. Women I would work with, go to dinner with, whom I would fall in love with. One of those women would eventually be my wife. On a quiet night, I would tell my wife about Cindy Sherman.

The rain fell. I felt a sudden jolt of regret. I looked into the sky, into the treetops. *God, what had I done? What if I made a mistake?*

Then I was okay and I knew I'd done the right thing. I

had the paper to worry about now. And colleges. And my senior year. I blew my nose with a napkin I found in my pocket. I thought about my grade for AP History. I had to write a paper about the ancient Athenians.

I put the napkin back in my pocket. I kicked a piece of asphalt. Shattuck Road was old, crumbly on the sides; there were potholes left over from winter.

I imagined Cindy going home, pulling into her driveway, going inside. Her family would be there, her parents, her dog Rodney, her little brother Ben who had asthma. She would tell them what had happened, and they would try to comfort her. Her mother would hold her in her arms while she cried.

*What were you supposed to do?* How could you love people when this was what happened? My first love was over. One of the most important parts of my life was gone. Cindy Sherman was the first person I loved like my own family. I would have died for her.

Which made me cry again. But I was running out of tears. Even with the rain dripping down my face, I was drying up. I was crying myself out.

At home, my front door was unlocked. It was after midnight. I let myself in and took off my dripping coat. My mother was in bed, asleep. So was my sister. The lights were off.

I went upstairs to my room. I kicked off my wet Nikes and dried my head with a towel. I sat on my bed. My own room looked strange to me: my Portland Trailblazer blankets, my Radiohead poster. There was a picture of Cindy on my desk. I quickly hid it in a drawer. I put on a dry T-shirt. I couldn't take a shower because my sister's room was next to the bathroom and it would wake her up.

So I went to bed. I knew I wouldn't sleep but I did it anyway. I was still damp, still cold, but gradually my blankets warmed up. I lay on my side. I curled into a ball. I stared at the wall, my eyes wide open, blinking in the darkness.

# 3

I was late to school the next morning. I got off the Metro bus and walked quickly across the front lawn, scanning the campus for any sign of Cindy. Fortunately, she was a sophomore and in the frosh/soph wing. I was a junior, in the junior/senior wing. So we at least had that separation.

I had come late on purpose, so I wouldn't have to see anybody. I made my way to my first period journalism class, which was in the *Owl* office. The halls were empty, except for a few people still running to class. I felt very alone all of a sudden. I'd had a girlfriend my entire junior year. Now I was just me.

At the *Owl*, people looked up when I came in. Bryce Whitman was right in front. He sneered at me. He always did that. I had beaten him out for the editor position.

My friend Kirk was at the back table, listening to his Walkman and writing a music review. He was bobbing his head and bouncing his knee like he does. The sight of him made me feel better. I sat next to him. I opened my notebook and tried to look busy. I watched Kirk write. I had planned to wait to tell him, but the weight of it was too much. I tapped his shoulder. "I broke up with Cindy," I mouthed.

"What?" he said, slipping off his headphones.

"I broke up with Cindy," I whispered.

He clicked off his Walkman and looked around the room. He leaned over to me. "Are you serious?"

I nodded. And for a moment, unexpectedly, I thought I might cry.

"Dude," said Kirk, looking around some more. "When?"

"Last night. At the basketball game."

"When did you decide to do that?" he said.

I couldn't answer. Tears were coming into my eyes. I had to look away for a second.

"Dude," he said. He found some napkins in the desk drawer. He gave one to me.

I blew my nose. "Where's Mr. Owens?" I asked.

"I don't know. He was here at the start of the period."

"Did he say anything about me not being here?"

"Nah, he's cool."

I stared at the back of Bryce's head.

"What happened with Cindy?" whispered Kirk.

"I don't know," I said. "I thought we needed to talk about things but once it started . . . I couldn't stop it. It snowballed."

Kirk watched me. "Where is she? Is she at school today?"

"I guess so."

"What did she say?"

"Not much."

"Man," he said, shaking his head.

"I know."


Peter Daley was in my AP English class, third period. He sat with me in the back. He leaned across his desk. "Kirk told me," he whispered.

I stared forward.

"Dude, what happened?"

I didn't answer.

"Are you out of your mind?" said Pete. "Cindy's one of the hottest girls at this school."

Mr. Thompson, our teacher, was late. People started to talk. One girl stared at me from the front row. She had a look of deep concern and disapproval.

I sighed heavily.

"This is huge," said Peter Daley. "This is going to affect everything. You and Cindy, you guys were like *the couple*. Everyone was into you guys."

I stared forward.


At lunch I sat at my usual table. Kirk was there and Peter Daley and Bob Hollins. All my guy friends knew by now. It was weird. It *was* affecting people. Girls would walk by and stare at us. At me. They did not look happy.

"You're never going to get another girlfriend at this school," Peter Daley said under his breath.

"Don't be an idiot," said Kirk. "Of course he will."

"You think so?" said Pete. "Look at these girls. They are *pissed*."

"So what," said Kirk. "They'll get over it."

"Somebody else will get her now," said Bob Hollins, a little too loudly. "And you hadn't even done her yet."

"Don't be an asshole," said Kirk.

"You guys still hadn't . . . ?" whispered Peter Daley.

I shook my head.

"Dude!"

"You sleep with them, and *then* you break up with them," said Bob Hollins.

"I heard Cindy was trying out for cheerleaders," said someone further down the table.

"You broke up with a future cheerleader?" said Peter. "Do you understand what that means?"

"Check it out," said someone else. "You know how Hillside had those hot new cheerleader uniforms? Their principal banned them."

"Did you hear about that chick from Glencoe?" said Bob Hollins. "Who got implants? They were going to ban her."

"Why can't our cheerleaders get implants?"

"Our cheerleaders suck."

"They're the worst."

"Except for Sasha Dillon."

"She's awesome."

"Dude, did you see that sweater she was wearing yesterday?"

"Did you see that other chick, what's her name . . . ?"

They went on like that. I ignored them. Kirk did too. That's why he was my best friend.

After lunch I saw Tara. She was Cindy's best friend. She was in the main office. I didn't know what she was doing there. She saw me, but I looked away.

After AP History, Dominique Taylor was waiting in the hall across from my locker. She was with Gabby Greenberg. They were both sophomores, like Cindy. They were also two of the most popular girls in our school.

I went to my locker and they came up behind me.

"We heard you broke up with Cindy," said Dominique, gravely.

I nodded that I had.

"What happened?" said Gabby.

I shrugged.

"You don't have to tell us anything," said Dominique. "But since you'll be the editor of the paper next year and everything. . . ."

"What does that have to do with it?" I said.

"Well, just . . . "

"We wanted to get the story from you," said Gabby.

They weren't kidding.

"It wasn't working out?" said Gabby.

"I don't know," I said.

"Cindy's crushed you know. She ran out of second period in tears."

"Everyone's talking about it," added Dominique.

I looked at the two of them.

"Did you not know that?" asked Dominique. "About second period?"

"No, I didn't."

"She's very upset," said Gabby.

"I'm upset too," I said.

"Why are you upset?" said Dominique.

"Because I care about her," I said. "I didn't want to hurt her."

"But you did," said Dominique. "You totally did."

"She *loved* you," said Gabby.

I put my stuff in my backpack. I shut my locker. They stood watching me.

I walked away.

— — — — — — — — — — — — — — — 4

My dad was in Alaska that week. He's a geologist. My mom was busy too, so it was easy to avoid talking about the breakup at home. My sister Drea was around but she had sprained her ankle playing softball, so she was watching TV all week with her foot on a chair. She was only in eighth grade anyway, at the middle school, so she hadn't heard about it yet. But she would.

Then, on Saturday, my dad came home and we had a family dinner. My mom made pork chops and pineapple, which everybody liked. We ate in the dining room. I kept quiet. My sister told a long story about a neighbor girl who got her learners permit and drove her dad's car into the back of their garage, smashing their trash cans and her brother's bike.

"How's the college stuff?" my dad asked me, ignoring Drea.

I was sending away for college applications, Harvard, Yale, that sort of thing. You were supposed to get all the literature and be thinking about it the summer before your senior year.

"I've got most of it," I said.

"How's that history paper going?" asked my mom.

I nodded that it was okay.

"This is the semester that really counts," my dad told me. "In terms of the colleges."

"I know," I said.

My dad ate his pork chop. Drea drank her milk.

"How's Cindy?" said my mom.

"She's . . ."

Drea was the first to notice something wasn't right.

"She's okay," I said.

"Bob Hollins's mother told me he's applying to Lewis and Clark," said my mom. "He's thinking about pre-law."

"What's up with Cindy?" said Drea, watching me like a hawk.

I didn't answer. But my mother picked up on it. My dad

did too. They all waited for me to say something.

"Nothing. We . . . " I felt my face flush. "We sort of . . . broke up."

"Oh dear," said my mom.

"Oh," said my dad.

Drea said nothing. She stared at me.

"What happened, honey?" said my mom.

I tried to chew. I couldn't. I put my fork down. "Nothing. We just. We were . . . talking about stuff . . . and then . . . "

"Oh, honey," said my mom.

"No, it's all right," I insisted. "It's for the best, you know, with all the changes and everything. She wants to be a cheerleader."

"Cindy does?" said my mom. "That's odd. She doesn't seem like the type."

"I know. It's weird. And she's hanging out with Dominique Taylor and Gabby and those people."

"Who are they?" asked my dad.

"Dominique Taylor," explained my mother, "is Howard Taylor's girl."

"Oh," said my dad, respectfully, Howard Taylor being one of the Taylor family who ran the North Region Lumber Company. They owned half of Portland.

"So she's getting new friends?" said my dad, still not quite understanding.

"Yeah and you know . . . she's not . . . I'll be doing the paper and all that."

Drea was staring at me. She wasn't buying any of this.

"Maybe it's for the best," said my mom. "She wasn't the

brightest girl. Is she even thinking about colleges?"

"She's only a sophomore," I said. But it was true, Cindy would go to the University of Oregon or some normal place. She wasn't interested in good colleges.

"She was so nice though," said my dad. "Whose idea was it to break up?"

"It was yours," said Drea, sharply. "It had to be."

My mom spoke up. "Well, it's hard trying to have a girl-friend and study and do everything you need to at your age."

My dad dabbed his mouth with his napkin. My mom went back to her meal. Drea stared hard at me. At seven dinner broke up. Dad went to the TV room to watch *The News Hour with Jim Lehrer.*

Drea came to my room later. I was reading about the ancient Athenians.

"Max?" she said, knocking on my door.

"*What?*" I said, as if I didn't want to be disturbed. But the ancient Athenians weren't very interesting. Somewhere I had gotten the impression that they wore togas and had wild sex festivals or whatever. All they did in this book was discuss atoms and the nature of virtue.

"I need to ask you something," she said. She came into the room. She sat on my bed.

"What?" I said.

"What happened with you and Cindy?"

"It's personal."

"But I need to know."

"Why?"

"Because what if it happens to me?"

"If it does, then you'll know."

She sat there, staring at me from my bed. "Did she cry?"

I looked into my book. "Yes, she cried."

"Why did you do it?"

I sighed. "I don't honestly know. I guess I felt like it was time to move on. And I have other things to worry about now."

"Do you like somebody else?"

"No."

"Can I ask you a personal question?"

"I'd rather you didn't."

"Was it something about sex, was she doing it wrong?"

"That's none of your business," I said.

She remained sitting on my bed. She said, "Did you know Sonya Taylor did a list of all-time Evergreen couples and you guys were number two? Tony and Jessica were number one. Of course."

"Good for them," I said into my book.

Drea remained on my bed.

"Is that all?" I asked.

"But didn't you guys love each other?"

I sighed with annoyance.

"But didn't you?"

"Yeah, we did," I said.

"So how could you break up?"

"It happens. I don't know. I have to get back to this."

"Okay," she said. She got up and limped toward the door. She didn't have her crutches.

"How's your foot?" I asked, without looking up.

"It's okay."

"Listen," I said, finally turning to her. "For future reference. This kind of stuff is private. Okay? Especially sex stuff."

She looked at me. "But I need to know about things. Who else am I going to ask? Mom?"

"Ask your friends. That's what they're there for."

"But none of my friends have been in love."

"They will be."

"How do you know? It doesn't happen that often." She stood staring at me, letting her words sink in.

I went back to my book. She limped out of the room.

Late that night I found the April poem. It was called "The Waste Land" by T. S. Eliot. I flopped on my bed and read a little:

> *Your arms full, and your hair wet, I could not*
> *Speak, and my eyes failed, I was neither*
> *Living nor dead, and I knew nothing,*
> *Looking into the heart of light, the silence.*

I stopped reading. I couldn't take it. I thought, *I just broke up with the only girl I will ever love.* I let the book drop off the side of the bed and turned sideways toward the wall.

— — — — — — — — — — — — — — — — 5

The next weekend there was a party of some people Kirk knew from Hillside High School. Hillside people were famous for their wild parties. I didn't feel very social, but Kirk thought it would do me good.

The party was okay. Not great. There weren't that many people. There was one guy from Hillside I knew from their debate team. Julie Hewson, whose house it was, had fooled around with Kirk at summer church camp when they were in seventh grade. She was pretty punk or goth or whatever, as was Kirk. She was annoying though. She kept screaming at her friends to bring back the vodka.

I talked to the debate-team guy for a while. Then I went into Julie's mom's room. Julie and two other girls were bouncing on the bed to a Rob Zombie song. They were being pretty crazy. One girl's breasts were falling out of her dress.

But her mom's room was depressing. There was nothing in it, just bare white suburban walls, a bed, a lamp someone had just broken. The closet was open, and you could see all the cheap clothes. The whole house was sort of cheap. It was like a divorced woman's suburban house where she lived with her punk daughter. Which was exactly what it was.

So we left. We drove around. We went downtown. Everyone was cruising Broadway, even though it was supposedly illegal. These dumb girls would drive by and look at you and

21

start laughing, or they'd want your cell phone number so they could call you. We didn't have a cell phone. Some guys from Glencoe High stared at us like they wanted to fight. Then a carload of girls pulled up and one of them made tongue gestures at Kirk. But when he rolled down his window they started screaming and drove away.

Then I saw a red Ford Explorer. My heart jumped into my throat. Could Cindy be down here? Could she be looking for me? But the Explorer had a ski rack. And it wasn't Cindy's license plates, which were DHT 198.

I was still freaked out though. "I don't want to drive around anymore," I told Kirk.

So we parked and went to this café Kirk knew about that had an air hockey game in the back. It was kind of a kid hangout. Kirk got his favorite drink: the Depth Charge. It was like three espressos inside a hot chocolate, or some insane thing.

We got our coffees and sat in a booth. We watched people. We chewed on our stir sticks.

Then this girl and two guys walked in. Everybody looked at them. The guys had makeup on and were dressed like rock stars. The girl had dyed black hair and red lipstick and a lacy blue dress.

"Check these guys out," said Kirk quietly.

I already was.

Despite their outrageous clothes, they were very reserved. They ordered their coffees and paid and maneuvered through the tables to an empty one next to our booth.

That's when they noticed us. They noticed Kirk, actually. He was wearing his cool orange T-shirt and his hair had been dyed red and was growing out. Not that he was as cool as them, but at least he was in the ballpark.

No one was going to say anything though. We sure weren't. But then the girl spoke. She looked over at Kirk and said, "Hello."

Kirk froze. He couldn't look at her. I kicked him under the table. He said, "What's up?"

The guys grinned at each other. The girl smiled. "Not much. What are you guys doing?" she said.

"Nothing. Hanging out," said Kirk.

"Where have you been tonight?" said the girl.

"We went to a party."

"Really? Was it fun?" she said. She seemed genuinely interested.

"It was okay."

"We never get invited to parties," she said to the two guys. They both laughed. We laughed. But then Kirk couldn't think of anything else to say.

They talked among themselves. Kirk and I tried to talk too, but Kirk kept staring at the girl.

When they left, the girl said to Kirk, "It was so nice to meet you. If you go to any more parties you should invite us."

Kirk was so flustered all he could say was, "Okay."

"My name is Eleanor," she said, more to me now. She held out her hand. I shook it.

When they were gone Kirk was like, did she really want

to go to a party? Should he have asked for her phone number? Should we chase them and get it? He got another Depth Charge and we sat and thought about it. Then he wanted to walk around and see if we could find them again.

We couldn't. So we went home.

# 6 - - - - - - - - - - - - - -

The following week, I saw Tara in the hall at school. She was in the junior/senior wing again. I looked away, thinking she would too, but she didn't. She came toward me.

"Hey Max," she said.

"Hey Tara," I said, cautiously.

"You don't have to avoid me, you know."

"No, I know."

"Cindy has some stuff she wants to give you."

"What stuff?"

"Your *Owls* sweatshirt. Some CDs. I told her I'd give them to you."

"Oh."

"I have them in my locker. You can come over after last period. She'll be gone by then."

"Okay."

She stood watching me. "So what happened?"

I shrugged. "We broke up."

"It was kind of sudden wasn't it?"

"I don't know. I've never done it before."

Tara stared at the notebook I was carrying. "She's kind of having a hard time."

"Is she?" I said, looking at Tara for the first time. "Is she all right?"

"She is but last week . . . that was bad. She had to go home one day. I had to talk to Mr. Brown." Mr. Brown was our principal.

"Wow," I said.

"She's pretty upset."

I nodded.

Tara sighed. "The thing for her is, she doesn't know what she did. Or what happened. Or what changed. You didn't give her any reasons."

"Yeah," I said.

"I mean, if you don't know, you don't know."

I nodded more.

"Anyway," said Tara. "So come get your stuff last period."

"Okay," I said. "Thanks."


*The reason I broke up with Cindy.* I thought about it on the bus going home that night. I got out my notebook. I wrote it out:

*Reasons I broke up with Cindy:*
*1. We weren't talking.*
*2. It was getting painful to see her.*
*3. I felt tired when I was around her, relaxed and*
   *energetic when I wasn't.*

4. *I was going to be the editor of the paper next year and I needed more time.*
5. *I wanted to go to a good college, she didn't.*
6. *She ignored me at Gabby's party and shook up beer cans, and it seemed like she wanted to be friends with Gabby and Dominique.*
7. *She wanted to be a cheerleader which was a typical spur-of-the-moment decision which didn't make any sense. I was sick of trying to pretend like she was actually going to do things like that when I knew she wouldn't.*

It was hard, because these really were the reasons, and yet when I read them back they seemed totally ridiculous.

That night I started my paper about the ancient Athenians. I struggled through half a paragraph. It was terrible. So I went downstairs where Drea was watching TV. I sat on the couch for a while. I guess I wanted to talk to Drea about Cindy. But when I saw her sprawled on the floor, flipping through the *TV Guide*, I thought what's the use? She wouldn't know. I didn't know.

That week I studied a lot. I worked on my paper about the ancient Athenians. It was about how they didn't have any technology but somehow they created a great civilization. How did they know so much? They knew what molecules were, without microscopes or computers or anything. Just by looking at things and thinking a lot, they realized matter was made up of millions of infinitely small particles bouncing around.

I also did a story for the *Owl* about the basketball team. That sucked though, because I had to write about the game I went to with Cindy when we broke up. I was afraid she'd read it and think that's what I was really paying attention to that night. But what could I do? I had to write it, it was an assignment.

That article led to another problem, because Bryce had a long piece about Ultimate Frisbee in the same issue, which created space problems. He always wanted to do alternative sports or skateboarding or extreme mountain climbing. He and I were filling in as dual sports editors, but we never got along. I always said you had to do the main sports: football, basketball, baseball, because that's what most people cared about, especially parents.

Bryce didn't want to do sports, but the sports guy had transferred out midyear and so we got stuck doing it together. Mr. Owens, who was our *Owl* advisor, decided that. It should have been Charlotte's call. Charlotte Volk was the present editor-in-chief, my predecessor, but she never did anything. She had been accepted early decision to Berkeley, so that was it for her. She left the paper to us.

The real problem was that Bryce was going to be the official sports editor next year. Not only did he not get editor-in-chief but he also lost to Kirk for editor of the Student Life section, which was culture and music stuff. So he ended up in sports, where he was not happy.

Like I said, all of this started when the old sports guy transferred out. The good news was that same Christmas an Australian girl transferred in. Her name was Jill St. John. She was kind of a hippie, but she was a good writer, and she always had stuff about students against this or that, or Greenpeace or a demonstration she'd been to. She was also really pretty. The first day she came into the *Owl* office I was shocked how beautiful she was. But she dressed in work shirts and baggy jeans and she wouldn't shave her armpits, so people didn't think of her in terms of being a babe.

Anyway, that's what I was doing. Studying, doing *Owl* stuff, getting back to normal. One night I shot baskets with Drea, who was walking around on her ankle and trying to get it back enough to play softball. She was such a good hitter they didn't care if she couldn't run fast. They just wanted her to stand there and swing the bat.

It was funny, Drea and I. I was the boy, but I was the brainy one. She was the jock. I got all the attention for college stuff and academics, but you should have heard the softball coach on the phone when she sprained her ankle. He needed her. He needed her bad.

- - - - - - - - - - - - - - **8**

Two more weeks passed. I studied a lot. I didn't do much socially. But then, on a warm weekend in May, Kirk dragged me to a party at Carla Benning's, who was one of the most popular seniors.

It was one of those big spring parties. There were people from every class. I was worried that Cindy or Tara might come, but they didn't. Kirk and I hung out in the driveway and shot baskets under a floodlight with Peter Daley and Bob Hollins.

Bob Hollins had recently surprised everyone by daring to ask Gabby Greenberg to the prom. She had agreed to go "as friends," but he was still really proud of himself and bragging to everyone. He was going to get some cocaine from his older brother. I guess he thought that might impress her. Maybe it would.

After basketball Kirk and I cruised through the house. We found our way to the keg in the back yard. Then we saw some girls going into the guest house above the garage. We could hear voices coming from the windows. We decided to check it out.

Inside, there were about seven or eight people sitting on the floor while two freshmen girls were supervising a game of spin-the-bottle. I couldn't tell if they were drunk or what. Everyone was kind of laughing at them. The first girl was being really bossy. Her name was Lydia, and she kept changing the rules so she could kiss who she wanted.

Kirk immediately joined the game. Lydia's friend Jane joined it too—she must have thought Kirk was cute. Lydia spun the bottle for her and stopped it with her foot so Jane would get Kirk. So off they went, into the corner. Everyone thought that was hilarious. No one was taking it seriously. Kirk and Jane came back. Kirk wiped his mouth on his shirt sleeve.

Meanwhile, Lydia made me sit in Kirk's place, and when I did, another freshman girl said, "Hey, you're Max. You broke up with Cindy Sherman."

I didn't answer. But Lydia seemed to take note. She looked at me for a second. Then she spun the bottle. It went to another boy, but Lydia kicked it until it went to me. So I had to make out with Lydia.

I did it. Kirk was cracking up. I went to the corner with Lydia and she threw her arms around me and gave me an exaggerated, slobbery kiss. She pressed herself against me until I finally had to pull her arms off my neck.

Meanwhile the game had stopped. Jane said, "Come back Lydia, who's going to spin the bottle?"

"Can't you spin your own bottle?" said Lydia. But she

liked being the center of attention, you could tell. She kissed me once more and ran back to the others.

The game continued. Jane got me. So we made out. Then while we were still in the corner Lydia made Kirk come with her into the same corner so we were all making out together. My back was bumping up against Lydia's, while I was kissing Jane. Then Lydia called out, "Switch!" and we switched partners. So I was with Lydia again. Everyone thought this was very funny.

Kirk and I eventually escaped the guest house and went back to the main party. We found Peter Daley and Bob and told them about spin-the-bottle. They laughed. Bob said, "Lydia Kresch, that girl's a freak!"

A few minutes later, Lydia and Jane appeared in the kitchen. They were obviously looking for us. Lydia walked boldly toward the four of us. She grabbed Kirk and pulled him away and whispered something to him.

Kirk came over to me. "They want us to come back to the guest house with them."

Pete and Bob both laughed and gave us the thumbs-up.

"What do they want?" I asked Kirk.

"Dude, what do you *think* they want?"

"But they're freshmen."

"So? They're girls, they're cute."

"They're fifteen."

"Yeah and we're seventeen," said Kirk. "So what?"

"I just don't think it's a good idea."

"Hey. You need this, okay? Don't think. Just come."

I looked at Peter Daley. He nodded I should go. Bob Hollins pushed me forward.

Kirk and I followed Lydia and Jane up the stairs to the guest house. Without anyone there it seemed bigger.

Lydia and Jane suddenly seemed nervous. They were arguing about if Brad Pitt was a Sagittarius. Kirk saved the day by grabbing Jane and kissing her. As soon as Lydia saw that, she grabbed me. It was the same as before, the slobbery kiss, her pelvis pressed into mine. At least she smelled good.

She led me into a little bedroom. She turned off the light and we sat on the bed and kissed some more. It was okay, but she was still trying too hard. At one point she paused dramatically and whispered, "Do you want me to take off my shirt?"

"No," I said.

"*No?*"

"That's right. No."

She pulled back. "But why not?"

"Because."

She stared at me in the dark.

I tried kissing her again but she stopped me. "You went out with Cindy Sherman," she said.

I didn't answer.

"Is it because of that?" she asked.

"No. I just don't want . . . to get involved right now."

"So it *is* about her."

"No, it's not. I don't know you."

"All right," she said. She kissed me again. She pressed herself against me and then, in an absurd fake-sexy voice, whispered, *"Do you want me to take off my pants?"*

I pushed her back. "If I didn't want you to take off your shirt, why would I want you to take off your pants?"

"I don't know."

"It doesn't make sense. It's not logical."

She looked at me with an odd stare, like she wasn't hearing anything I said.

"Am I right?" I said. "Does it make sense?"

"What do you want me to do?"

"Nothing. Jesus."

"It's about Cindy Sherman, isn't it?"

"No! It's not about Cindy Sherman."

"You guys were in love. That's what everybody says."

"Why are we talking about this?"

She scooted closer to me. "I think Cindy Sherman is beautiful."

"That's it," I said. I got up.

"No," she said, grabbing my hand. "I mean that as a compliment. To you."

I pulled my hand free. "I'll see you later."

# 9 - - - - - - - - - - - -

By mid-May I had all my college applications. My mom and I went through them. We practiced on the Stanford application: filling out the info, going over the essay questions. We even got the envelopes ready for the recommendations. The essay questions were the hardest part. I wanted to write my main essay about fighting forest fires, because I planned to do that when I turned eighteen. And I had done a big article about smoke jumpers earlier that year for the paper.

My mom didn't like it. She wanted me to write about my uncle whom I worked with over the summer. He owned a garden shop and he was deaf. She insisted this was the thing the good colleges would like. She had read a book about it.

So I gave in and wrote a practice essay about my deaf uncle. But really, there wasn't much to say. He was deaf. He pointed at things and made gestures. It was not a big deal. It wasn't as exciting as parachuting into a forest fire.

Afterward, during my homework, I got this strange urge to talk to Cindy. I wanted to tell her about the college stuff. And about other things. I even wanted to tell her about Lydia Kresch. It got so bad I felt an actual pain in my chest. Residual connectedness I guess.

I ended up talking about colleges with Jill St. John. Besides being in journalism class, she had started sitting at the *Owl* table at lunch. Even though she was Australian, she knew all about American colleges. Reed was going to be her first choice, or Berkeley. We talked about it for an hour after school one day.

Later, Kirk said I should ask Jill St. John to the prom.

Another issue I was dealing with: I didn't have a car. I didn't even have a license. And I was seventeen.

Kirk had a car. Pete Daley had a car. Cindy could have her parents' Ford Explorer whenever she wanted it. Tara wasn't quite sixteen yet, but she would get her older sister's Toyota. Gabby Greenberg had a Lexus. Dominique Taylor wasn't sixteen either, but you knew there'd be a new Cherokee or something waiting for her in the driveway with a big bow around it. Even environmentally conscious Jill St. John had an old Honda Civic.

I had nothing. My mom always said, "We live right on the bus line." That was true. I could get to school in ten minutes. I could go downtown. I could go to Woodridge Mall. But people still thought it was weird. Drea said if she were me she would fight to the death for a car. She would refuse to eat. She was mad at me for letting our parents get away with it. It would make it harder for her.

The reality was, Cindy had got the Ford Explorer in December when she turned sixteen. So in a way, I *had* had a car. It was nice riding around in the Explorer. I missed it. Not that I would regret breaking up with Cindy over something like that. But I noticed it. I noticed it when it was pouring down rain and I was standing by myself at the bus stop.

- - -

I started thinking about the prom. I had to go. The future editor of the *Owl* had to go to the prom.

But who could I ask? I guess I had been hoping I could still somehow go with Cindy. That seemed like the right thing to do. No one else agreed. Not Kirk or Peter Daley. Even Drea thought it was a terrible idea, and that Cindy would say no anyway.

But that made me think: what if someone else asked her? It was possible. I hadn't even thought about her with other guys. Part of me was okay with it. She would need to move on. I wanted her to be happy. But actually seeing her in public with another guy? I couldn't take it. I really couldn't. It would destroy me.


On Thursday, Lydia Kresch and Jane were waiting for me outside the junior/senior wing.

That was not good.

"Hi," I said.

They didn't answer. Lydia gestured for Jane to leave. That was obviously the plan. But Jane didn't want to. Lydia scowled at her. She almost kicked her. Jane finally left, and Lydia announced that she wanted to talk to me. I said okay. I was going to the *Owl* office. She could walk me there.

"So, uhm," she said, following beside me. "You know on Saturday, at Carla's party?"

"Yeah?"

"I'm sorry for saying that stuff about Cindy Sherman."

"Yeah?"

"You're not supposed to talk to guys about their exes. I read an article about it in *Glamour*. I won't do it again."

"Good."

"Do you forgive me?"

"Yes."

"Okay. But the thing is," she continued. "Since you guys did break up? I was wondering if you had someone to go to the prom with?"

"Oh."

"I could go with you," she said.

"But you're a freshman."

"That doesn't matter. I'm a good prom date."

"Yeah?" I said. "How many proms have you been to?"

"Uhm . . . "

"Zero?" I asked.

"I went to the ones at my middle school."

"That doesn't count," I said. "I'm not going anyway. And if I do, I already have someone."

"Who?"

"Jill St. John. From the paper."

"Do you like her?"

"We're friends," I said. "That's all I want right now."

"Can we do something else though? Go to Woodridge Mall? Or a movie?"

"I don't think so."

"But what about last Saturday?"

"What about it?"

"You know. What we did. In the guest house."

"We played spin-the-bottle."

"No, the second part. In the bedroom."

"That was a continuation," I said. I was walking quickly.

She hurried to keep up. "What's a continuation?"

"It's when you continue to do something you were already doing. They don't count as two separate things."

"But they *were* two separate things."

"Well," I shrugged. "If you thought they were, you should have made that clear."

She hurried to keep up. "But we kissed. And we talked about stuff."

"It was still part of the spin-the-bottle game."

"But what if I don't agree?"

"It doesn't matter. In a continuation it has to be specified."

She looked confused. She stopped. She wanted me to stop too. But I kept walking.

"Listen, I'm late," I said. I turned and walked backward for a few steps. "I have to go."

"But—"

I turned forward. I kept walking.


At home that night our house was dark. My mom was some-where. My dad was in Alaska. Drea came down to the kitchen to show me the food Mom had left us.

She sat with me while I ate. Her middle school friends were still asking about Cindy and me. What had happened? What had Cindy done? What made a boy stop loving a girl? Especially a girl as perfect as Cindy Sherman.

"I wish I knew," I said.

After I ate, I rinsed off my dishes. Drea started back

upstairs. I stopped her. "Do you know a freshman named Lydia Kresch?"

"I've heard of her."

"What have you heard?"

"Not much. That she's boy crazy. That she's crazy in general."

"Who says that?"

"I don't know." She shrugged. "Everyone?"

# 10

I asked Jill St. John to the prom, "as friends." She accepted, and on prom night I put on a very uncomfortable rented tux and took the bus to her house. An hour later we were picked up by Bob Hollins and Gabby Greenberg. Bob had got a limo somehow. He also had some cocaine. So he spent most of the night running off to the stairwell or sneaking back to the limo with Gabby and some other not-too-bright girl I didn't know. Gabby also had a flask of something, which she kept dropping. Everyone was sure she would get busted, but somehow she didn't.

Dominique Taylor went with Bryce, whom she ditched immediately. She spent most her time trying to get Gabby away from Bob. At one point she and Gabby disappeared for almost an hour, leaving Bob waiting around, sniffling and complaining about how much he'd paid for the cocaine, and how pissed he'd be if he didn't "get any." Which he didn't.

The prom itself was pretty bad. It had an eighties theme. The band was four old guys who kept saying how cool it was that people were into the eighties again. I wasn't into the eighties. Jill wasn't either. She thought people were morons in the eighties. "It was the Reagan era," she said. "It was one of the worst times in history."

Kirk didn't come. He didn't believe in proms. Peter Daley was there with Melissa Brant, whom everybody liked but nobody ever asked out. She looked really good though, and Pete and I talked about how people looked so different at proms. The standard babes looked less cute, and then some of the not-so-cute girls suddenly looked amazing.

Dominique Taylor looked good, though. She always looked good. And then she had a big party after. I assumed we'd go, but Jill didn't want to. She thought the Taylors were evil, being in the lumber business. That was fine with me. I didn't want to spend any more time with Bob or drunk Gabby in the limo. So we bailed and went to Chuck's Original Pancake House with Pete and Melissa. There must have been a prom somewhere else in the city, because at Chuck's other people were wearing tuxedo pants and prom dresses.

That night, at home, I took off my shirt and shoes and sat at my desk. That's when I realized: if I had stayed with Cindy, I would have just lost my virginity. With Cindy. Whom I loved. We would have been each other's first. It would have been perfect. It would have been just like it should be. Now what was going to happen? Now who would it be?

I had read somewhere that your first sexual experience set the tone for the rest of your life. If your first time was an act of love you would grow up to be a person who had solid relationships and a good marriage. But if you did it with some drunk girl at a party, someone you didn't care about, it would screw you up forever. You'd end up as some bald guy cruising the bars for divorcees the rest of your life.

On Monday at school everyone was talking about the prom and Dominique's party. Bob was telling everyone he had made out with Gabby, but people were saying she had passed out, so it didn't count.

It was all kind of stupid, and Kirk and I snuck off campus and went to McDonald's for lunch. It turned out he had had some interesting adventures of his own that night. He had gone downtown to a new all-ages dance club called Agenda. It was the grand opening. He was hoping that Eleanor, the girl we met at the Air Hockey Café, might be there, and she was. Kirk said when she saw him, she came right over and started talking to him. They talked and hung out and at one point went outside and sat on the sidewalk against the building. She told him about her life, how she ran away and she was living on the street for a while and how her mom lived in L. A. and was addicted to painkillers. Then Eleanor, Kirk, and one of her punk guys walked around. The punk guy's name was Brian Brain. Or so he called himself. Brian Brain was giggling to himself the whole time. Kirk thought he was on drugs. They went to the Air Hockey Café, and then Eleanor saw a girl she was having a feud with and ran off. That left Kirk and Brian Brain together. Suddenly, Brian Brain could talk. Like out of the blue they started having this totally normal conversation. Kirk even said, "How come you couldn't talk before?" And Brian Brain said, "Sometimes my meds don't hit me right."

Kirk explained to me that "meds" were antidepressants or antisuicide drugs. It all sounded very dramatic and underground and kind of fun.

# 11 — - - - - — — - - — — - - - -

My dad came back from Alaska again. We had a family dinner, and afterward he wanted to see my college applications. He noticed I wasn't doing debate next year. I told him I wouldn't have time, and anyway, the debate people were geeks. "Geeks go to good schools," he said.

Then we talked about the summer. I wanted to fight forest fires in eastern Oregon. Someone had told me you could lie about your age and get on the crews. My dad wouldn't even consider it. He had met with my uncle Jack, who wanted me to work at his garden shop again, like I did the previous summer. I really wanted to fight fires. I had also considered working with a group of volunteers that Jill St. John had told me about that go to Central America and build bridges and houses and stuff, but I had flaked on that when I heard you

42

had to get twenty-six vaccinations. So the result of that conversation was I would work at my uncle Jack's garden shop.

There was one positive to that plan: I would need a car. There were no buses to the garden shop and Uncle Jack didn't want to pick me up every morning, like he did last summer. So everyone decided I should get my license. In fact my dad was a little baffled I didn't have it already. I had to remind him that he and Mom *didn't want me to get a license*, but they claimed they never said that. Anyway, the final plan was I would get my license and my dad would buy a third car which I would use for the summer and for school next year. This meant I would also have to drive Drea to school, but I could live with that.

That week I got my learners permit and my dad took me driving. It was pretty easy. I didn't tell my dad, but Kirk had occasionally let me drive his car. And so had Cindy. Cindy had *a lot*. And a Ford Explorer was a lot harder to drive than my dad's Camry. But I pretended I didn't know how, and my one week crash course in driving was completed without incident. It had to be. My dad was flying back to Alaska in a week.

The night before he left, my dad pulled into the driveway in an old Honda Accord. This was my car. Well, not *my* car, the "third car" as my parents were careful to say. And they weren't going to activate the insurance until the end of May. I would still be taking the bus to school. But I didn't care. I loved the Accord. I put an old KROC sticker I had on the bumper. I sat in it late at night.

- - -

All that was left was to go to the Woodridge Mall DMV and get my license. My mom left me there and went shopping. I was sitting in the waiting room when Dominique Taylor walked in with her mother. Dominique had just turned sixteen. That day. I was seventeen and a half. It was a little embarrassing.

Dominique came over and said hi. She introduced me to her mom as the future editor of *The Evergreen Owl*. Mrs. Taylor said, "How nice." She was hot though, for a mom, and very fashionable. It was weird to see them together. You could see how similar they were.

Her mother left and then it was the two of us. We made some small talk. Then Dominique thought for a second. "Wait," she said. "So you're just now getting your license? But you're, like, seventeen?"

"Yeah," I said.

"Why so late?"

"I didn't really need it. The bus goes right by my house. It only takes ten minutes to get to school."

"And Cindy had a car."

"Yeah," I said, casually.

"How's that going?"

"Fine, I guess."

"No regrets?"

"Well . . . "

"I heard she went out with Charlton Hughes," said Dominique.

"She did?" I said, surprised.

"I don't know what happened. He asked her out though. I know that."

I nodded. But it hurt. It hurt a lot. And Charlton Hughes. He was this annoying rich kid.

"She has to go out with someone someday," said Dominique, trying to be nice.

"Yeah," I said. "I guess."

I took my test. I got a hundred.

When I left, Dominique was still there. She stopped me. "I'm having some people over this weekend," she said. "A pool party thing, if the weather's okay."

"Oh."

"I wasn't going to invite you because I thought Cindy might come. But she can't. So if you want to."

"Oh. Okay."

"One thing though, don't bring that guy Kirk."

I looked at her.

"I mean, he's nice and everything. But . . . you know. . . ."

Kirk was my best friend, but he was a little too weird for people like Dominique. It made for difficult situations sometimes.

I nodded. "Okay," I said. "What time?"

# 12 - - - - - - - - - - - - - - -

"Charlton Hughes?" Kirk said. "I hate that guy. He's *the worst*."

"I know."

"What's Cindy dating him for?"

"He probably drove her around in his BMW. She falls for stuff like that."

We were driving downtown in Kirk's car. It was a beautiful day. It was the end of May now. All the windows were open.

"And Dominique Taylor told you this?" asked Kirk. "And you believe her?"

"Why wouldn't I?"

"Charlton Hughes," grumbled Kirk. "I hate that guy's hair."

"I always worried about Cindy in that way," I said. "That people could manipulate her."

"Ah forget it," said Kirk, accelerating. He looked into his side mirror and changed lanes. "Summer's coming. We gotta find new girls. Julie Hewson's been calling me."

"What does she want?"

"To take her clothes off."

"I don't want to see Julie Hewson with her clothes off."

"But she's got cute friends. She can hook us up."

I watched a strip mall pass on the right.

"You do want to get hooked up, right?" said Kirk.

I didn't answer.

"Dude, I know what you're thinking," said Kirk. "But Cindy's gone. You gotta think about other options. And you gotta get laid. We're going to be seniors remember. In three months."

Downtown, we walked around the record stores. We checked out 360 Vinyl which was where all the techno kids hung out. It was a very cool place. Kirk wanted to get this new German group, but he couldn't find it.

Then we got coffees at the Air Hockey Café. We always went there now, to maximize our chances of running into Eleanor. Kirk got a Depth Charge. I got a regular house blend. We were mixing in sugars when Eleanor walked by. She was across the street with another girl. Kirk saw them. He freaked. He left his Depth Charge on the condiment counter and ran out the door. I followed, trying to be a little more reserved.

Kirk caught up to them. Eleanor looked amazing. She had these huge black sunglasses, and this sexy dress and old dirty Converse tennis shoes. The other girl was hot too. Her name was Danielle. She was older and kind of aloof, though you could tell she enjoyed watching flustered Kirk try to talk to Eleanor.

Kirk was a mess. In all this time he still hadn't got Eleanor's number. This was his chance.

"Like, uhm, what are you guys doing this weekend?" he asked.

"Agenda on Saturday," said Eleanor. "A famous DJ is coming from London."

"Oh yeah, right, yeah, do you guys need a ride, should I call—"

"Need a ride?" scoffed Danielle. "I live right down the street."

"But I mean, like you, Eleanor, do you, should I call—"

"I can walk," said Eleanor, slickly removing a cigarette from her tiny purse. "We'll meet you there."

"Okay," said Kirk. "That sounds good but maybe I should get your—"

Eleanor lit her cigarette. She was looking at me now. "Who are you?"

"Max," I said.

"Oh, you're Max. Kirk was telling me about you."

"Not too terrible things I hope," I replied. I felt a sudden formality come over me. Eleanor, it occurred to me, was a very formal person.

"No, not terribly terrible," she said with her cigarette in her mouth.

"Why don't you give me your number," Kirk finally blurted. "And that way we can, you know, you can tell me what's up, or we—"

"You can call me at Danielle's," said Eleanor.

"Don't call my house," said Danielle.

"Oh," stammered Kirk. "But what—?"

"We have to go now," said Eleanor. "Ciao."

"Oh, yeah, *ciao*," said Kirk.

We stood while they walked away.

Later, Kirk told me that "ciao" means good-bye in Italian.

- - -

At the end of May, the new issue of the *Owl* came out. Jill St. John had a piece about a tree spiking she did in Washington State. Tree spikers inserted metal rods into old growth trees so that loggers couldn't chainsaw them. The article started:

> *My fellow earth defenders looked at each other in silence as the Jeep rolled through the black night. Our call to defend our mother had come. We were ready now to do battle with the Earth Rapers. For many of us, it was our first action against those who would destroy Nature's greatest glories to line their own pockets.*

Nobody thought it was particularly controversial, but Mr. Brown, our principal, got some calls from parents. There were some e-mails, and even some letters. And then Dominique Taylor's dad called. That was a big deal.

So Mr. Brown called a meeting with the *Owl* staff. Charlotte Volk was there. We rarely saw her these days, since school was out in two weeks. But Mr. Brown really came down on her. Apparently there was a district policy that said you couldn't have articles about students doing anything illegal in a student paper. Charlotte totally caved. My guess was she had never read the article. Mr. Owens was also there and apologized. Jill of course was indignant. But she didn't say anything.

In the end, we promised not to do it again. Or I promised. It was an important moment because that was when the paper shifted from Charlotte to me. Mr. Brown got mad at Charlotte. But in the end, it was my promise that he wanted. I was the one he had to deal with now.

# 13 - - - - - - - - - - - - - -

I went to Dominique's pool party. Peter Daley came with me. When we got there, Dominique and Gabby were in swimsuits, sunbathing on recliners. They looked like movie stars. Some other girls were there. A couple of people were swimming. Bryce was there, playing Frisbee with Charlton Hughes. I avoided looking at them.

Dominique didn't get up. She told us to go inside and get drinks or whatever, and to change. Her house was a total mansion, though I pretended I didn't notice. Most people had been there before. I hadn't.

We went swimming. The pool was big and they actually had a diving board, which no one has anymore. People would run off the diving board and do funny poses or try to catch the Frisbee someone would throw from the sides.

More people came. Some freshmen I didn't know. The beautiful people of the frosh/soph wing. Peter and I and Bryce started a water polo game, which was fun except the ball kept getting knocked out of the pool and the girls wouldn't get it for us. Peter kept having to get out and crawl in the bushes to retrieve it.

Then Lydia appeared, standing at the side of the pool. Jane was there too and some other girls. They went inside and changed and came out in their bathing suits. I focused on the game. I stayed in the pool.

After water polo, I was sitting with Pete and Bryce in the sun and Lydia came over and sat with us. Lydia wasn't super cute but she looked pretty good in a bathing suit. For a freshman.

"Hey Max," she said.

"Hey," I said, without enthusiasm.

"I didn't know you were friends with Dominique."

I shrugged.

Pete got up for a second. Lydia took his place.

I frowned.

"Don't worry," she said to me. "I'm not going to bother you."

"I'm not worried."

Bryce went to get something to drink, leaving us alone.

"I just wanted to say hi," said Lydia. "Is that all right?"

"I guess."

"I know you don't like me."

"It's not that I don't like you," I said.

"You liked me for one night."

"Listen, I told you—"

"I know. It was a *continuation*." She smiled at me. "Can you do me a favor though?"

"What?"

"Put some sunscreen on me?"

I did it. She turned away from me and held her hair so I could do her neck.

I put some on. She arched herself while I did it. She stuck out her little breasts.

"Under the straps," she said.

I smeared some under the straps.

"And can you rub it in?" she said.


Despite the Lydia weirdness, it was a pretty great party. There was music and the sun and the pool. People were really nice, and nobody threw anyone in the pool or did anything too stupid. It was the power of Dominique. She brought out the best in people.

Even after the sun went down, people stayed. Dominique would put people's stuff in the dryer and give them a bathrobe. The Taylors had like twenty bathrobes, just for the guests. They were so comfortable we were all wearing them. Peter and Bryce and I started a "bathrobe poker game."

Then Lydia came over to me and asked if I would come with her.

"Where?" I said, looking at my cards.

"Just come," she said.

"Why?"

"I want to show you something."

"What could you possibly want to show me?" I said.

The other guys started snickering.

"Just go with her, for chrissakes," said Bryce.

I folded my poker hand and went. Lydia led me into the laundry room. She was also wearing one of the bathrobes. There was a nervous smile on her face.

In the laundry room there were two dryers running. It was loud. It was steamy and hot.

"What is it?" I said.

"I need you to feel something," she said, grinning.

"That's not funny."

"No, not that," she said. She turned to the dryer. She opened it. She pulled out some shorts. "Are these dry?"

"These aren't even yours."

"They're Jane's. Do you think they're dry?"

I touched them. "Yes. Whatever. Is that all you wanted?"

She threw her arms around my waist. She just grabbed me. And held me. It was so sudden I couldn't stop her. And once she had me, it sort of felt good. She was a girl. She was soft. She smelled nice.

But she was Lydia Kresch.

"All right, that's enough," I said, prying her arms off.

"Why can't you give me a chance?" she said.

"Because."

"Can't you just kiss me?" she said. "I know you would like me if you gave me a chance."

I kissed her. Once. I don't know why. I guess there *was* something about her I liked. She was so reckless. She had no fear. It was kind of cool. In a way.

After the kiss she stepped back from me and reached for her bathrobe belt. She started to untie it. At first I didn't understand. Then I saw what was coming: she was naked under the bathrobe and she was going to drop her bathrobe on the floor.

"Oh no you don't," I said. I grabbed her around the waist, pinning her arms to her side. She struggled but I kept my hold on her. I picked her up and carried her into the hall. I carried her sideways into the main room, her bathrobe still on, her bare legs kicking. I dropped her roughly on the couch.

Everyone was staring. I went back to my card game.

"What was that all about?" said Pete.

"*Freshmen,*" I sneered.

"*Freshmen,*" everyone agreed.

"They don't know their place," said Bryce, looking at his cards.

"When I was a frosh, we had respect," added Pete.

# 14 - - - - - - - - - - -

Despite my preemptive actions, people still talked about the Lydia bathrobe incident at school on Monday. How could they not? Lydia and me alone in the steamy laundry room. Lydia naked under her bathrobe. Me carrying her down the hall and dumping her on the couch. All of it taking place at Dominique Taylor's which was the best possible setting for any scandal.

It *was* Lydia Kresch, so people understood it was probably her doing. But they still looked at me funny. First I broke up with Cindy whom everyone adored. Now I was involved in this Lydia craziness. This was not what people expected from Max Caldwell.

In the hall Monday morning someone said, "Wild weekend Max?" Some other people whistled and laughed. I ignored them.

Jill St. John also heard about it. During first period she would barely talk to me. I didn't know what that was about. She and I had been working on an article about the corrupt company our cafeteria bought its food from. She gave me the latest printout and walked away.

Kirk was in the corner listening to his headphones. I sat with him for the rest of class.


At lunch there was more talk, more looks. Peter Daley and Bryce were telling everyone what happened.

Kirk was there. Finally he listened to the details. "Wait," he said to me. "This was at Dominique Taylor's? She had a party? And all you guys went?"

"I wanted to tell you," I said. "But she didn't want me to invite anyone."

"How did these idiots find out?" he said, gesturing to Peter and Bryce.

"I don't know," I said. "I was going to call you."

Kirk got up and walked away, leaving me to tell the story yet again. But it sucked about Kirk. Everything sucked at that point.

- - -

I found Kirk after school and he gave me a ride home. "Dominique didn't want me to invite anyone," I told him.

"Whatever. I wouldn't have gone anyway."

"Did you go to Agenda this weekend?"

"Yes."

"Did you see Eleanor?"

He stared straight ahead. "Yes."

"What happened?"

"I thought she liked me. I guess she likes a lot of people."

"But that's for the best, right? I mean, her being a runaway and living on the street and stuff. You can't go out with someone like that."

"Why can't I? I'm not getting invited to Dominique Taylor's."

"Yeah but look at who she hangs out with. Brian Brain, he's a total freak."

"Yeah, and what am I?"

"You're not him."

"At least Brian Brain stands for something. At least he's not afraid to piss people off."


At home my mom was waiting for me.

"Maxie?"

"Yeah, Mom?"

"Can you come in here a second."

I went.

My mom was reading the paper in the living room. I stood in the doorway. I put my hands in my pockets.

"Do you know a girl named Lydia Kresch?" she asked.

"Oh, *great.*"

"Come in here. Sit down a minute."

I came in. I sat.

"Her mother called me," said my mom.

"Lydia Kresch's *mom* called *you?*" I said. It was unbelievable. "What did she say?"

"She said Lydia told her you were her new boyfriend."

"I'm not."

"That's what I said. I said I didn't think you had a girlfriend."

"Good."

"Her mother said they suspected as much. They said Lydia's quite a handful, but they try to check on things and keep her out of trouble as best they can."

"Well they should, because she's *a lot* of trouble."

My mother watched me closely. I avoided her gaze.

"Are you . . . physically involved with her in some way?" she asked.

"No," I said. "I mean, not . . . "

"Yes?"

"No, I mean, a little. She grabs me and stuff. It's terrible. It's embarrassing."

"Her mother hinted that there was a physical aspect to it and they were concerned."

"We kissed. Nothing else."

"They thought there must be some reason she thinks you're her boyfriend."

"She's crazy. That's all it is. Everyone knows it. Ask Drea."

"Okay. Well. I believe you."

I looked at my hands.

"I do think," said my mother. She did one of her polite smiles. "That this young woman is someone to steer clear of."

"*Obviously*," I groaned.

"But if it's so obvious why did you get involved with her?"

"Because I'm stupid, what do you want me to say?"

"Don't get mad at me," said my mother. "All I'm saying is, you can get yourself into trouble in situations like this. Even a small thing, when it's with the wrong person, can be very hurtful to your reputation."

I said nothing.

"You've worked very hard," said my mother. "You have accomplished a lot. And with college applications coming up. . . . Nothing a girl like this can do for you will be worth it. Do you understand that?"

"Yes."

"All right then."

I started to leave.

"And I don't want to hear from her mother again," warned my mom.

I went to my room. I threw my stuff down and threw myself on my bed. I lay there for a long time.

- - - - - - - - - - - - - - - **15**

Jill St. John had organized a hike for the *Owl* staff, the last
week of school. Charlotte Volk had okayed it. No one else
paid any attention. I totally spaced it. A lot of people did.
Then suddenly there it was, June sixth, a Sunday, the day of
the *Owl* hike. There were actually eleven people on the list.
Jill St. John had reserved a school van and everything.

So we went.

Kirk and I sat in the back. Jill and Bryce sat in the front.
Mr. Owens drove. Charlotte Volk couldn't come of course. A
couple of the freshmen who would be on the staff next year
were there. This kid Kevin who had an annoying voice and
tended to correct your grammar. Another girl, Rebecca, who
no one had ever seen before. She had thick glasses and
stared at Kirk and me like we were the great gods of high
school journalism. Sophomore Maria Sanchez, who disap-
proved of everything, sat across from us, to better keep an
eye on things.

The hike was okay. It was kind of a weird group. Kevin
was full of scientific comments like, "It is actually not true
that you can always determine accurately the age of a tree
by counting its rings."

There was a tall sophomore, Josh Markowitz, who kept
walking into low-hanging tree branches. He was like six foot
two and totally uncoordinated. He had forgotten to bring

water or candy bars or whatever, so everyone had to give him some of theirs.

One good thing: Jill St. John, who had kept her distance since the Lydia bathrobe scandal, had no choice but to talk to me now. She and I and Kirk walked together. She was showing us stuff: clear cutting, erosion, how you could check the leaves for acid rain. It was pretty interesting. The problem for me was my dad was a geologist. He sometimes worked for Exxon. So it always felt like if I got involved with environmental issues it would look like I was doing it against him. I mean, I cared about that stuff. I was taking Environmental Science next year as one of my electives. But I didn't want to get too anti-whatever while I was still living at home. It would be too much against my father. At college, I could get more involved in stuff. Especially if I went back east where I'd be far away.

We hiked for several hours and then stopped for lunch at a meadow on a high bluff. Kirk and I had both grabbed frozen burritos and frozen sandwiches at 7-Eleven at the last minute. They were pretty gross. Of course Jill St. John had an organic cucumber sandwich with sprouts and vegan mayonnaise or whatever.

We sat on the grass and looked at the landscape and ate. Jill sat next to me. That's when I had the thought: *Maybe Jill likes me.* She went to the prom with me. Maybe she wasn't mad about the sexism of the Lydia scandal, maybe she was *jealous*.

And maybe I should like her. She was sort of perfect. The

problem with Cindy was she just went along. She was into whatever anyone else was into. Maybe with someone like Jill, who was so opinionated, things would be more equal. And that would keep it fresh. It would keep me on my toes.

Plus, Jill was beautiful. I watched her eat. She had thin wrists and her fingers were long and perfectly shaped. She was elegant. She would be as good looking when she was old as she was now.

A slice of cucumber fell out of her sandwich. I picked it up. It had a little dirt on it which I brushed off with my finger. "Do you still want it?" I asked.

"Sure," she said. She took it. She ate it. She smiled.


On Monday, Lydia was waiting to ambush me outside the junior/senior wing. I saw her and immediately changed direction. But she followed. She ran and caught up with me.

"I'm not talking to you," I said before she could speak.

"Why not?"

I walked faster. I didn't look at her. I didn't speak. Then I said, "Please don't follow me around, it's embarrassing."

She stopped. I kept going.


Later that week I went to Woodridge Mall. I had to get Drea something for her birthday. Since it was at the beginning of summer, people always got her lame summer stuff like cheap swim goggles or trendy sunblock. I was trying to think of something more interesting. Like a candle or maybe a book.

I was walking around, kind of enjoying the mall. It was air conditioned and bright and probably had that fake air they pump in that makes you buy stuff. Also, the middle schools must have let out, because there were a million teenyboppers running around. It was fun to watch them. In a year or two they'd be Evergreen students and *Owl* readers.

Then I ran into Cindy. Like right into her. She was sitting at a table outside the food court. I practically knocked it over.

I didn't know what to do. I couldn't *not* say something. "Cindy," I said.

She looked up.

"Hey," I said. I swallowed. "What's up?"

She was as horrified as I was. "Nothing," she said.

"Oh," I said. I could feel my face turning red. "I . . . I was looking for something . . . for Drea. . . . "

She stared at me.

"Yeah," I said. "So . . . how are things? What are you doing over the summer?"

"Nothing," she said. "Working at my dad's office."

"Oh," I said.

She stared at me.

"Yeah, I guess I'm going to be working at my uncle's garden shop this summer."

She didn't answer. She looked different. Or maybe the way she looked at me was different. Her face had a strange misery in it. It did not light up like it used to.

"Okay, well, I guess I'll go now."

"Okay," she said.

I turned and walked away. I found an exit and stumbled down the stairs and out of the mall.

# Part Two  Summer

– – – – – – – – – – – – – – – **16**

Summer came. I went to work at the garden shop. It wasn't
exactly parachuting into forest fires but it was better than
bussing tables at the Copper Penny, which was what Kirk
was doing. And my uncle was cool. He wasn't like my dad, he
was very laid back. He made a lot of money without doing a
lot of work. And you never minded going to the shop. It
smelled good, especially in the morning, and the work was
easy: water the plants and hang out and help people. You did
need to know what care the different plants required. And
you had to wear a rubber apron and these tall rubber boots
that made your feet sweat.

Also, the shop was attached to this fancy grocery store
called Rotter's in the West Hills. So there were a lot of cute
girls around. And rich old ladies and rich guys in convert-
ibles talking on their cell phones.

And of course my uncle was deaf, so you had to do gestures and sign language with him. I didn't really know sign
language, but I had picked up a little the summer before.

He'd write things down if it got too complicated. It never did though. Like I said, he was pretty cool.

Then one day, Pete came by and invited me to play tennis with his cousin and this other girl he liked. I had my car, so I drove to meet them after work. There was still some tension with my parents about the so-called "third car," like was I really allowed to drive it wherever I wanted? Drea kept telling me it was my car, and to act like it was and not give in to Mom and Dad. Drea got very angry when I didn't defend my rights.

So I drove to the tennis courts. They had big overhead lights with bugs flying around in them. Peter and his cousin and the other girl were already there. They were playing two against one so I joined right in. I was on his cousin's team, Ashley Cole was her name. The other girl was Corinne, and you could see why Peter liked her. She was tall and blonde and really pretty in that obvious way Peter likes. Ashley was more dark. She wasn't that pretty, but she tried hard at tennis.

Afterward, we got Cokes from the machine and sat at a picnic table. Peter was into Corinne, but I couldn't tell if she liked him back. Ashley and I made small talk. She asked me where I wanted to go to college. I told her back east and she got very excited. She wanted to go back east too. She said, "I have good PSATs and I'm going to be the editor of my school paper next year."

I said, "You are? So am I."

So then we *really* started talking. Like what it was like

to be editor and how we got it and what it would be like next year. She went to Portland Episcopal School, which was private and had a really good paper. I had seen it. But Evergreen had a good paper too, since we were the newest school in our district and had tons of money and all new computer stuff. She knew about our computers and talked about them in an odd way, like it wasn't fair, like we had an unfair advantage. It was an oddly competitive thing to say. Especially since Evergreen was a public school.

But in general we were both psyched to meet. I suggested we hang out and compare notes over the school year. She agreed. Or I thought she did. It was hard to tell. It had been weird being her tennis partner. She had gotten mad when I missed shots.


But Ashley did want to hang out. In fact, she invited me to dinner at her parents' house the next week. I found myself wondering if she might like me. Maybe we could go out. We had so much in common. And she was obviously smart. We could be a power couple.

At dinner, her mom and dad were all over me. Like what did my parents do and why hadn't they heard of me and how wonderful Peter Daley was (they were related to him). It was a little intense. After dinner her dad took us to the basement and showed us his train set. He had model trains going all over the place. It was kind of weird. He was fifty years old. Ashley was embarrassed too, but she was probably used to it.

That night I drove home in the "third car." I took the

long way home, through the hills, which were lush and green and overgrown in early summer. I rolled down the windows and cranked the radio. Even if Ashley didn't work out, it was good to be out in the world, meeting new people, being a man about town.

# 17 - - - - - - - - - - - - - -

I often read during my lunch break, and one day I started a book Jill St. John recommended called *The End of Nature*. It was about how we have taken over nature's role as the caretaker of the planet. How nothing is really natural anymore: the fish all come from fish hatcheries, the trees are all planted by man and harvested. Even wild animals are "managed."

It also said that at the rate we burn gas and cut down trees we would fry the entire planet in the next fifty years. Probably sooner. It pretty much said we were doomed.

I kept reading it all that day. I read it at intersections driving home. I read it in the TV room that night.

Drea was watching *Charmed*. I asked her, "Do you think the world will end while we're alive?"

"I hope not."

"This book says it will. It says the greenhouse effect is changing the air so fast that within our lifetime the whole earth will change."

"That's not good," said Drea.

"Doesn't that bother you?"

"Ask Dad, he probably knows."

Later, before bed, Drea came into my room. She was in her pajamas, her toothbrush stuck in her mouth.

"Do you know Bryce Whitman?" she asked.

I was on my bed, still reading *The End of Nature*. "Yeah," I said. "What about him."

"A girl at my school likes him. Sonya Taylor."

"Dominique's little sister?"

She nodded.

I didn't say anything. Bryce and Dominique's sister. That would be interesting.

"What's he like?" asked Drea.

"He's going to be the *Owl* sports editor next year."

"Sonya's already gone out with two guys from Evergreen, and she's only an eighth grader."

"Who else has she gone out with?"

"Charlton Hughes."

I looked up from my book. "*The* Charlton Hughes?"

Drea nodded with her whole body. "She supposedly did stuff with him," she said, brushing her teeth.

"Recently?"

"Before school let out. They went in his sauna."

"Cindy went out with him," I said.

"He takes girls in his sauna and they do things with him."

"Like what kind of things?"

"I thought you didn't want to talk to me about stuff like that."

"Did he do *things* with Cindy?"

"How would I know? I don't go to your stupid school."


My dad was home that week, and on Wednesday I went to his study. He was doing something on his computer.

I sat down behind him, on the little chair he keeps there. I had my copy of *The End of Nature.*

"Dad?" I said.

"Yes, Max?"

"Is the planet going to fry in the next fifty years?"

"I hope not."

"What about the greenhouse effect?"

"The greenhouse effect is something to think about."

"Do you think about it?"

"I do," he said. "But it's not my field exactly."

"Are we going to fry?"

"I don't think so, son."

I sat there. I watched him work on his computer.

"Are you worried about it?" asked my dad.

"Yeah. Kind of."

"And what did Dr. Sorensen say about your pessimistic thinking?"

My parents had sent me to a psychologist when I was thirteen, because I had become obsessed with various forms of nuclear annihilation. I had seen *Terminator 2,* where they nuke Los Angeles. I had dreamed about it for months.

"Not to worry about things beyond my control," I answered.

"Is the greenhouse effect in your control?"

"I guess not. I mean, I could drive less."

"You don't drive at all. We just got the third car a month ago. Riding the bus all this time, you've been helping solve the problem, haven't you?"

"I guess."

"You've done your part. And if everyone does his part—"

"Dad, this book I'm reading says it's over. There's no stopping it. And once the oceans melt . . ."

"Max, I can't get into the specifics with you right this second. I have some very important work I'm doing."

I sat there. I watched his computer screen. He had a graph up. He punched some numbers in and the graph changed slightly. He punched in some other numbers and the graph changed back.

- - - - - - - - - - - - - **18**

Kirk came by the garden shop one afternoon. He told me about his recent downtown adventures while I watered the plants. Brian Brain was forming a band and had asked Kirk to join. The band would be called "Brian Brain." Kirk could play whatever instrument he wanted, but Brian Brain would be the singer. Then it turned out Brian Brain didn't have any equipment and didn't have a car or a place to practice. He wanted Kirk to drive everyone and to let them practice at Kirk's house. He also wanted Kirk to pay the deposit for the amps. Then, a couple of days later, they were all riding around in Eleanor's Volvo—

I stopped spraying. "Whoa, wait a sec, where did Eleanor get a Volvo?"

"It's her dad's," said Kirk.

"I thought she was a runaway and living on the street?"

"Oh no, her dad lives downtown. He has a really nice apartment."

"What happened to the whole runaway thing?"

"That's when she's between her mom's and dad's. She kind of hangs out, or floats around or whatever. She stays with Brian Brain. Her dad has a really nice place. He's the president of Willamette University."

I turned to Kirk. "He's the *president* . . . of a *university*?"

"Yeah, what's wrong with that?"

"Dude. She told you she was a runaway. She told you she lived on the street. Who knows what other stuff—"

"Who cares? She's awesome. We talked for two hours. I think she likes me."

"*I* think she's messing with your head," I said. I started spraying again.

"So she exaggerates a little," shrugged Kirk. He slipped his hands into his pockets. "Actually I sort of exaggerated some stuff to her."

"Like what?"

"Nothing big. Something about you actually."

"What?"

"I sort of told her you were going to Yale."

I stared at him. "Why did you do that?"

"Because. She was saying how her dad is the president of this big university. I thought it would impress her."

"Why didn't you tell her *you* were going to Yale?"

"She wouldn't believe that. She knows you're smart. She thinks it's cool that I hang out with someone like that."

I watered the little flower trays. "That's a dumb thing to lie about."

"It doesn't matter," said Kirk. "She won't remember. She doesn't remember half the things I tell her. Her memory is really bad. She says it's from doing acid when she was three. Her mom dosed her by accident."

A couple of days later, Jill St. John came by the garden shop. That was a surprise. I hadn't seen her since school let out. I was a little embarrassed to be caught in my apron and rubber boots. But it was great to see her. The nice thing about Jill was, whenever I was around her my best side came out. I became the best version of myself. I became polite and responsible and grown up.

I showed her around. I'm not sure she liked the shop. She said her friend worked at the Garden Warehouse at Woodridge Mall and ninety percent of what they sold was toxic chemicals. "Humans can't even have a yard without poisoning everything," she said.

- - -

That weekend, I went swimming with Corinne and Peter and Ashley Cole at the West Hills Racquet Club. Ashley and Corinne were both members. It was pretty posh there. All the girls were cute and all the dads were drinking Amstel Lights and walking around in their swimming trunks. The moms were talking on cell phones underneath big hats and sunglasses. Ashley was ignoring me for some reason. She was a difficult person, I was noticing. She barely talked to me, and when another guy she knew walked by, she ran after him and was gone for an hour.

It was still fun though. Peter Daley and Corinne were getting suntans. I had a lot of sunscreen on and I tried to explain that tanning was bad for you now with the ultraviolet light and all that. But they weren't interested. So I rolled over and started my new book. It was another Jill recommendation, *The Monkey Wrench Gang*. It was about these guys who blew up bulldozers to stop the destruction of the wilderness.

# 19

The summer deepened. I started wearing flip-flops to work. As the days got hotter, I went in at seven A.M., which was good because it was quiet then and Rotter's was just opening and there was a good hour or so before people started coming. It also gave me a chance to get a latte from the little espresso cart outside Rotter's. A guy named Sam ran it. He was only nineteen but he was a real go-getter. He and his older brother had espresso carts in three different shopping centers. They could make sometimes eight hundred dollars a day, per location. This cart was the best though; it was a gold mine. They had raised their prices fifty cents. Sam said the Rotter's crowd didn't even ask what things cost. They handed you a five and stuffed whatever you gave them back into their pockets.

That hadn't been my experience exactly, but it was fun to hear Sam talk about his various business ventures. He was going to open a Mexican restaurant as soon as he got his credit situation straightened out. He said there was a ton of money in it because the basic materials were so cheap. He and his brother had tried a sidewalk burrito stand a couple of years before and had cleaned up until the city wouldn't renew their vending license. They hadn't bribed the right people, he said. I didn't know if he was joking when he said things like that. But whatever, the coffee was good.

One night after work I met Kirk and Eleanor and Brian Brain at the Air Hockey Café. It was a really hot night and we walked around aimlessly and ended up in a park, sitting in the grass. Brian Brain wanted to get beer, but he had no money. Kirk and I gave him some, mostly to shut him up. Then Eleanor wanted Kirk to go with Brian Brain to the store. Kirk didn't want to, but she insisted. She said Brian would get lost or lose our money.

So then it was just me and Eleanor. That was weird.

She sat there and stared at me for a while. I picked at the grass.

"*Max*," said Eleanor, not asking me anything, just pronouncing it.

"That's my name," I said. I didn't like the way she made Kirk go with Brian Brain. And Brian Brain was getting on my nerves too. He was always whining about something.

"Kirk really looks up to you," said Eleanor. "You're like his big brother. I thought you were older than him."

"No, we're the same age."

"Do you feel responsible for Kirk? Since he looks up to you so much?"

"No, we're just friends."

"Because he would do anything you told him."

"No he wouldn't. He might do anything *you* told him."

"He does like me, doesn't he?"

I nodded.

"You don't like me as much," she said.

"I don't know you."

"You think I'm . . . what?"

"I don't think anything," I said. "Trust me. I have other things to worry about."

"Like what?"

"Normal things. School."

"But you're so smart. You're going to Yale."

"I'm *applying* to Yale," I corrected her. "I haven't actually been accepted anywhere."

She looked up at the night sky. "I'm going to apply there

too. My school record isn't so good, not as good as someone like you. But I have connections."

"That might work," I said.

"It wouldn't really be fair though. And I probably wouldn't like it anyway."

"You don't seem like the type."

She smiled at me. "There must be some pretty girls out at Evergreen High."

"They're all right."

"You don't have a girlfriend there?"

"No."

"That's odd. I would think you would be a very desirable boy."

I shrugged.

"If I was a nice girl in the suburbs, going to a nice high school, I would like you."

"But you're not a nice girl from the suburbs, are you?"

She smiled and leaned back in the grass. "Like if I was in the marching band," she said mockingly. "Or chairman of the glee club. Or if I was on the chess team or the cheer-leader squad, and wore a big pink sweater around my neck. I think I would probably fall in love with a boy named Max. Who was going to Yale and was the editor of the paper. You would be the perfect boy." She grinned.

I picked at the grass.

"Wouldn't you be?" she said. She was daring me to look at her.

I looked at her. I let my eyes lock into hers and we stared

at each other. Complicated things passed silently between us: possibilities and warnings and challenges, and also a kind of mutual respect. It was an interesting standoff.

Then Kirk came back with Brian Brain. They couldn't find anyone to buy them beer.

# 20

Fourth of July weekend I got invited to go fishing with Peter Daley, Bob Hollins, and Bob's dad. We would camp out in a desert canyon in eastern Oregon. I had a little trouble getting the third car for a two-night trip, but my mother finally gave in. My dad was in Alaska.

I left work early on Friday. It was a three-hour drive through the Cascade Mountains, and I got there about dusk that night. Mr. Hollins was a serious fisherman, and when I arrived the three of them were spread over several miles along the bank. I had my dad's fishing pole and some salmon eggs and a bobber, so I was okay. It was cooling down after being a very hot day. The river was running fast and quiet.

Eastern Oregon is high desert, dusty and rocky, with hard dirt flats and tall rim-rock cliffs that drop into canyons like the one we were in. There's sagebrush and rattlesnakes, and sometimes a cow will come wandering along from one of the ranches. That's what people do there, raise cattle and farm. Also, the altitude is several thousand feet, so it's hot in the day, but at night it gets cold as soon as the sun goes down.

I went off by myself and fished. I caught two trout. It was weird, because I hadn't been fishing in two years, and it freaked me out to kill the fish, like to whack them over the head with a rock. Especially after the books Jill St. John had me reading.

Mr. Hollins and everyone came back to camp when it got completely dark. We got a fire going and cooked all the fish in a big skillet. That was awesome, eating the fish in the firelight. After dinner, Mr. Hollins let us have a couple of beers and we sat around, drinking and talking and staring at the fire. At one point I went into the sagebrush to piss and it was suddenly cold, in the dark, away from the fire. I shivered and looked up and there were so many stars, it was incredible, like a shotgun blast across the sky. I stood there for a moment and let it hit me: the space, the emptiness, the silence. Then I zipped up and hurried back to the fire where it was warm and there was beer and Mr. Hollins was telling jokes about prostitutes.

The next day we fished more. The big event of that day was that Peter Daley saw a rattlesnake and chased it and threw rocks at it until he killed it. Then he ran back and found Bob and me. He wanted us to come look. So we did. It was like a half mile through brambles and sagebrush and Peter Daley was running the whole time because he was so excited. When we got there—all cut up and out of breath—it wasn't even a full-grown snake. It was a little one, a baby. And

Pete had bashed its head in, so you could barely tell what it was.

It did have a rattle though, so we cut that off with Bob Hollins's knife. The skin was so tough, you could barely cut it. And it was now the hottest part of the day and there was no shade. We kept looking around in case any other rattle-snakes were around. What if baby snakes had mothers who would be protective? But nothing happened, except we sweated a lot and finally got the rattle off. Bob said we should take it back because you could skin them and make stuff out of them, like rattlesnake belts. But nobody wanted to touch the front of it. Even though its head was pretty much gone.

Later we got back to fishing, and just as it was getting dark I caught a fish. I thought I did. I started reeling it in but it got loose. But even after it escaped, the fish kept jumping around and freaking out. When I got the line in, there was something on the hook. It was his eye.

Peter Daley was up the bank from me. He asked me what happened, and I told him I had caught a fish's eye. He said, "Don't worry, fish can survive anything."

But later, back in camp, I was thinking what it would be like to be a fish and have your eye ripped out. The other fish wouldn't help you. They're all fighting for food, trying to get enough for themselves. And with only one eye, you're never going to get the food. Think how desperate you'd get, as you got more hungry. And probably from the moment you lost the eye you knew you were doomed. You'd be swimming around not seeing anything very clearly. And worrying about bigger fish catching you. You couldn't even kill yourself, unless fish have some special way they do that, like throw themselves up on the shore.

Maybe you'd want to swim off and die of hunger by yourself. Maybe you'd swim back to where you were born, to see things one last time. You might as well, no one else would want you around. Who wants to hang out with someone who has their eye ripped out and is dying of hunger?

When we had dinner, I could barely eat. I tried telling Mr. Hollins about the fish, but he just laughed. Everybody did. I was getting one of those stomach aches I used to get when I had to see Dr. Sorensen. I seemed to be getting those again, about global warming, and the paper, now about the fish. It was since . . . well, it was since I broke up with Cindy.

I thought about Cindy. I stared into the fire and imagined her sitting beside me or rubbing my head like she did when I was getting too worried about something. I hadn't thought of her lately, but now thoughts of her came flooding over me. Her smell and her hair and her body, and how it would feel to rest my head on her chest like I used to, like she was my mother and loved me absolutely and would do anything to comfort me.

I didn't want any beer that night. Peter told Mr. Hollins about the snake, and Mr. Hollins thought we should have brought it back. We could have skinned it. Bob said it was too small, it was just a baby, and then Peter claimed it wasn't, or if it was, how was he supposed to know? He was just trying to save his own life.

Bob's dad laughed. Everyone felt embarrassed for Peter. We were all pretty quiet that night.

# 21

When we woke up the next morning everything seemed okay again. It was early morning and cold, and we put on our coats and gathered around Mr. Hollins at the camp stove. He had some special peppers and cheese to put in our eggs. We had more fish too, which we fried in butter in the big skillet. We were hungry in a new way, in a raw way, like we weren't city boys anymore, now we were outdoorsmen, and we didn't care about hurting fish or snakes, we wanted to eat.

Eventually the sun reached the top of the canyon and it started warming up. We went off by ourselves to fish. Sort of. Peter wanted to stay near me, at least near enough to talk. It was okay though. We got bored fishing and talked about girls and colleges and sports. Peter wanted to write sports articles for the paper next year. I told him to do it. We needed dependable people. Bryce was going to flake, I was sure of it.

So that was fun. At one point I hooked a big trout. I actually had to play it a bit as I reeled it in. Peter waded over to help. When we got it in close we kept the trout in the water and unhooked it without touching it. We let it go and it vanished with a flick of its tail.

"That was a big one," said Peter.

"Yeah," I said.

"Should we have kept it?"

"We got a bunch."

"Yeah, we got a million."

Later Peter wandered upstream toward camp. It was getting very hot by then and the fish weren't biting, so I lay down in the shade. But then ants started biting me. I had to run into the water and brush them off. Then Bob Hollins came floating by, wearing his old straw cowboy hat. He had bailed on the fishing too. So I dove in and we floated on our backs and let the river take us downstream. It was very peaceful and quiet, though later I had a terrible sunburn on my face and we had to walk about two miles in wet tennis shoes to get back.

I drove the third car back to Portland that night. At first the three of us made a little caravan, Bob Hollins and his dad in their big F-250 pickup, Peter Daley in his dad's Suburban, and me in the Honda Accord. Eventually Peter stopped for gas though, and Mr. Hollins drove really fast, so then it was just me by myself.

I tried tuning the radio but you couldn't get anything while you were crossing the mountains. So I turned it off and drove. I could hear the wheels making that smooth sound on the pavement, the car engine humming, the heater blowing. Outside, the deep forests of the Cascade Mountains moved silently by, hiding their secrets, hiding their beauty and stillness from mankind. For now.

# 22 - - - - - - - - - - - - -

I was back at the garden shop at seven on Monday morning. I unlocked the main gate and put out the display pots. I put on my apron, my rubber boots. I walked around with my spray hose.

Sam arrived and got right to work on his cart, opening the drawers and cleaning his espresso machines. Everything had to be spotless with him. He was the most dedicated high school dropout I had ever encountered. Not that I had encountered any before.

The Rotter's employees began to dribble in. Rotter's didn't open until eight, but the cashiers would get their cash registers set up and then come outside and smoke or buy coffees from Sam.

At eight the first customers began to appear. One guy always came and got a cappuccino and a copy of the *New York Times*. He was always there at five minutes to eight so that he could get his cappuccino and literally walk through the sliding glass doors right when the store manager unlocked them.

After that the flow was pretty steady. They made a lot of money at Rotter's. Sam made a lot of money. My uncle Jack made a lot. It was all about the flow. People moving through, the money moving through. That was Sam's theory. Every morning he gave me a free coffee and a little lecture about how people spend money. How they were more cheerful in the morning, how it invigorated them to drop five bucks first thing. It woke them up.

That same day, just after lunch, Jill showed up. She said she was in the neighborhood and I had told her to stop by. . . . It was great to see her. I showed her these new miniature Japanese trees we had just got. She liked those a lot. I showed her some other stuff. I kept thinking, *I gotta ask her out*. But I couldn't seem to find the right moment.

Then she spotted the espresso cart. She wanted a latte, so she walked over to Sam's cart while I helped a customer. After that I went into the washroom and washed my hands and smoothed my hair. *I had to ask her out*. When I went back though, she was still at the espresso cart. I walked over.

Something was up. Sam and Jill were arguing. Or something bad had happened. There was serious tension. They shut up when I arrived. But Jill was really angry. Sam was standing there with that hard, cocky look he had. Jill pushed past me and went back to the garden shop. I watched her go. I looked at Sam. He just shook his head.

- - -

Jill left soon after, which worked to my advantage. It gave me an excuse to call her that night, which I did. I said I was sorry if Sam had offended her somehow.

"It's not your fault. He's just uneducated. He can't see past his own profit motive. Basically, he has the mind-set that's going to destroy the world: greed, selfishness, self-interest."

I listened to her talk. But in my head I was back to *I gotta ask her out*. The fact was, I had never technically asked someone out, someone that wasn't already my girlfriend. I waited for a gap in Jill's speech. When it came I went for it.

"Would you want to go see a movie sometime?" I said, wincing silently to myself.

She sounded surprised. Shocked, even. Then she took a breath and said she'd love to. We made a time. Saturday.


I was psyched. A real date. On Saturday. Kirk and I cruised Broadway on Thursday night to celebrate. Then we went to a little store Kirk knew about where the guy would sell you beer if you gave him five bucks.

So we drove around and drank beer. We ended up in Clairmont, which was Tara and Cindy's neighborhood. I knew Cindy was on vacation. Her family always went to the San Juan Islands in July. So I told Kirk to drive by.

The Shermans had a big house, surrounded by trees. I stared at it as we drove by. It was dark and empty looking. We continued down the block and then I told Kirk to go back. We needed a place to hang out. Why not Cindy's back yard?

We parked down the street, snuck across the Shermans'

front lawn, and crawled over their back fence. They had a table and chairs on their patio and we set our remaining beers on the table and put our feet up. They had a big back yard, which was good since we had to piss a lot. Also our beers had gotten shaken up climbing over the fence and when we opened new ones they foamed over.

After a while we got bored and Kirk started looking in the back windows. Kirk thought we should go inside. Maybe they had more beer. I knew there was an alarm. And it would be on. But Cindy had once shown me a basement window that wasn't hooked into it. It was hard to get to. You had to crawl under a rosebush. I don't know why I did it; to see if I could I guess. I squeezed under the bush and bumped the latch with my fist until it opened. Then I slithered through the small window space. And I was in.

- - - - - - - - - - - - - **23**

I knew where the alarm was. Cindy and I had dealt with it occasionally when her parents were out of town. So I knew how it worked and how to turn it off, which I did.

Kirk came in through the sliding glass doors. He went straight to the refrigerator. They had beer. We helped ourselves. We couldn't risk turning on the lights, so we wandered around in the dark. Kirk found a liquor cabinet and poured himself a shot of whiskey.

I went upstairs. For some reason I avoided Cindy's room. Instead I went into Janet's, her older sister. Janet was in college. I didn't know where she was that summer, if she was home or away. I didn't know what Cindy's little brother was doing that summer either. Ben Sherman. He had asthma and bad allergies, and they were always getting new air purifiers for him. His room was downstairs. So was her parents'. Her mother had come seen me debate once. I liked her mom. She was more normal than my mother, less worried about things. Her dad and I didn't do as well. He was always gruff with me, even though I did the exact thing a father would want: I loved his daughter without having sex with her.

I had never been inside Janet's room and found myself going to her bureau and pulling the top drawer out. There was underwear but nothing very sexy. I heard Kirk walking around downstairs. I looked around the rest of the room. For some reason I felt like I should be looking for something sexual. That's what you did when you were in an older girl's room, right? Instead, I looked at some pictures on her desk. There was one of Cindy. It was from years ago, before we went out. I couldn't see it too well in the dark.

I heard Kirk downstairs in the bathroom taking a piss. I thought we should leave before something happened. I went into the hall. Cindy's room was at the end. I didn't want to see it. But I was this close. Maybe for a second . . .

Her door was open. Her white comforter was on her bed. I had a sudden mental image of her getting dressed. We hadn't had sex, but we had done other things. I had seen her get dressed. I remembered her slender back, the back of her legs, her hair hanging forward as she pulled on her pants. That's when you know someone's really your girlfriend. When you're watching them wiggle into their jeans, when you're watching them snap their bra on like they do every day, like they'll do for the rest of their lives.

I moved into the room further. There was a new poster up, Sheryl Crow, who Cindy always liked. Also there was some stuff I hadn't seen before on her desk. On her bed table, where my picture used to be, there was a new cordless telephone.

The room was neat in general. I was careful not to touch anything. But I touched the bed. I sat on it. I could smell her. I moved my hand across the comforter. I slowly lowered myself until I was lying across it.

I could picture her then, in the dark, the two of us lying together. I should have slept with her. We should have been each other's first. And by breaking up with her not only had I doomed myself to sleep with someone else for the first time, I had done the same to her. I had sent her into the world to grow up on her own, to have to share that crucial moment with someone else, someone not me, someone who didn't love her like I—

"Max! Hey, what are you doing?"

I sat up. Kirk was standing in the doorway.

"Nothing, I was—"

"We better get outta here. Someone just drove by. Really slow."

I got up. We both went to the window and looked out. No one was there. The street looked quiet.

"Can you reset the alarm?" said Kirk.

I nodded. We snuck downstairs. I let Kirk out the glass door and reset the alarm. Then I crept down into the very dark basement. I stood on top of Mr. Sherman's exercise bike and crawled out the basement window. I think I kicked something, or knocked a picture off the wall. But I got out.

# 24 — - — - - - - - - - - - -

"Sam was a complete idiot," said Jill on Saturday. We were having a soda at the food court at Woodridge Mall. We had just come out of a movie.

"He's sort of working class," I said.

"He's not working class," Jill said. "Working class people have some idea of how the world works. If they're really working class they have ties to things. To the earth. They have to."

It sucked that Jill was so worked up about Sam. It didn't give me any openings.

"He always tells me about these businesses he's going to start," I said. "He's a real capitalist I guess."

"He's a conceited jerk. And then he was telling me that economics work themselves out and that people like me always appeal to people's emotions instead of their economic conditions. That is so condescending. What does he know about economic conditions?"

I nodded. I drank my soda. "He does have a lot of weird theories."

"His theories are bullshit. *He's* bullshit. I feel sorry for you that you have to work with someone like that."

I nodded. I drank my soda.

That's how it went: Jill and I struggling to find something to talk about, then a blast of Sam. Eventually we went back to our cars. She smiled and got into her Civic. We didn't make any further plans. We would be hanging out soon enough anyway. It was August; the first *Owl* meeting was just a few weeks away.

Going home, I imagined Jill in the future, married to a lawyer who defended the rain forests or poor people in the South or something. They would have a good life and have beautiful children and be happy and satisfied with themselves. Somehow I knew I could never fit in with that. I guess I didn't care as much. Or I cared about different things.

Meanwhile, Kirk was about to leave for Minneapolis to visit his father. His parents were divorced, so every summer he spent the last four weeks in Minneapolis with his dad. We had one last night to hang out. So we went to Agenda, the underage dance club. I still hadn't been. I was kind of nervous, but Kirk led the way. You had to wait in line and get patted down and go through a metal detector. Then you walked down this little corridor and into the big main room, which was all mirrored and lit up and pulsing to dance music. There were cute girls everywhere and slick city guys and super-weird people like Brian Brain, or goth chicks, or these really glammed-out fifteen-year-olds in glitter with their techno boyfriends. We went to the juice bar and got smoothies, and Kirk showed me the little rooms in the back where there were couches and places to make out, which people were doing all over the place.

There were also drugs around. You didn't actually see them, but you could feel them, you could feel the vibe of them. You could also tell how harsh people could be. Like if you did something uncool the people there would cut you down in a heartbeat. In a way that made it more interesting. It gave everything you did an added edge.

# 25 - - - - - - - - - - - - - -

On August tenth, I called Bryce to check on summer football. The team usually started practicing three weeks before the season. It was important to have an article in the first issue of the paper about it. People were into football.

Bryce hadn't even thought about it. "Football? It's August."

"Yeah," I said. "But you need to go to some practices. Talk to the coaches. See who the main players are going to be."

"Did they do that last year?"

"Of course. They do it every year. It's the football pre-view."

"Who usually does it?"

"The sports editor. You. That's what your job is."

"Oh," said Bryce.

"It's not that bad. Just go over there. It's easy."

"When does it start?"

"It already started. It's better to go at the beginning, then you can keep track of it."

Bryce did not sound enthused.

"Do you want me to go?" I finally asked.

"No, I'll go," he said. "I just have a lot of stuff to do right now."

"Like what?"

"Just . . . stuff."

After I hung up I thought about going there myself. But I couldn't start doing everyone's job for them.


*The Owl* was beginning to dominate my thoughts. I worried about the balance of the paper. The year before a lot of girls complained that there was nothing in it for them. There were tons of sports, tons of music reviews, but was there anything that, say, Dominique Taylor would like? Our two best girl writers were Jill St. John and the news editor, Maria Sanchez, but neither of them were into social stuff.

I e-mailed Ashley Cole about it. She told me they did this thing at her paper called "Crushes," where each week one student wrote about someone they had a crush on. There was a blacked-out profile with a question mark on it, and then a list of things the student liked about the "crush." It was very popular and of course everyone speculated about who the crush was and who wrote it, etc.

I liked that. Maybe we could do something similar. But who could we assign it to? Not Jill or Maria Sanchez. We had Rebecca, with the huge glasses, but she was impossibly shy.

Then I thought of Dominique Taylor. She was my target audience, why not ask her? I called her. I explained the situation.

"So you want me to write about someone I have a crush on?" she asked.

"No, no," I said. "That's an example. We need someone to think up a column, or a weekly piece, you know, something social, something girls would like. Maybe you could do like 'The Party Report.'"

"The *Party Report?* That sounds idiotic."

"Or . . . funny horoscopes. Or 'Couple of the Week.' Or best dating places."

"Sounds like you should do it. You've obviously been thinking about it."

"C'mon. You'd be perfect. You know everyone."

"Cindy didn't try out for cheerleaders," said Dominique.

"She didn't?"

"She was going to. That's what she told people last year. But Gabby said she didn't show up."

"Maybe she's still on vacation," I said.

"No, she's back. We saw her at the mall."

"How was she?"

"Tanned. But that doesn't mean anything."

The end of the conversation was that Dominique hated writing. But she would think about it. I told her we could get someone else to write it. All she had to do was think it up. And supervise.

— — — — — — — — — — — — — — **26**

At work, I was stockpiling stories for the *Owl*. I would think of them and run into the back and dry my hands and write them down. But then I lost a bunch of them when my uncle threw away an old envelope I had been writing on. I had to get organized.

I was also getting stomach aches and this thing my old psychologist Dr. Sorensen used to call "racing brain." That was when I would be thinking of so many things at once, and so fast, that I would make myself sick.

I went downtown after work one night and got an organizer notebook. It had dividers so I could put story ideas in one place, people's phone numbers in another, the *Owl* calendar in the back. The first *Owl* meeting was on August 23. I could hardly wait. I was so excited I had a stomach ache for two weeks straight.

My dad came back from Alaska. We had a family dinner. My mom was asking me about Uncle Jack and the paper and my dad was drilling me about my college stuff and then Drea started crying and ran away from the table. It was a total surprise to my parents. My mom went and talked to her. When she came back she said that Drea thought nobody cared about her. She was about to start high school and no one asked her questions or wanted to take her shopping or help her get ready.

I could have told them that.

I called Bryce. He still hadn't gone to football practice.

"I'll do it," I told him. "I did it last year. I know how."

"I'll do it," whined Bryce.

"You can come with me if you want."

"C'mon, don't be like this."

"I'm going Saturday in the afternoon."

I called Dominique. She didn't want to do anything for the paper. She said I should call Lydia Kresch, she was very social.

"No thank you," I said.

I went to the big Starbucks downtown after work, to do my final preparations for the first *Owl* meeting. I had my notebook, my latest list of story possibilities. I still needed some ideas for girls' stuff. I was also thinking I could just make Maria Sanchez social editor and let her figure it out.

I heard a rapping on the window beside me. It was Eleanor.

"Hey," she said through the window.

"Hey," I said.

She looked through the glass at the papers in front of me. This somehow aroused her curiosity. She walked around to the door and came inside.

I kind of didn't want her to. I felt like I had work to do. But really I didn't. I was writing the same things over and over. I had racing brain.

"Are you too busy to talk?"

"No," I said. "Not at all."

"I can't stay anyway," she said. She sat down across from me. It was weird because the minute she sat down I felt my body relax. Something about her was bigger than my problems.

"What are you doing?" she said.

"Getting my ideas together for the paper."

"That's right. You're the editor of your school paper. That's so sweet. That's so . . . seventies."

"Yeah," I said, grinning.

"How are you?"

"Me? I'm . . . I'm okay. Kirk is on vacation."

"So you're all by yourself."

"Yeah," I said.

"What are you doing this weekend?"

"Nothing."

"You should come to Brian Brain's house. He's having a party on Friday."

"Oh. I don't know. . . ."

She looked at the papers in front of me. "Look at how you work."

"I get sort of wound up," I said. "I'm glad you came by."

"Now I have to go," she said, looking at the clock. "But really. You should come by this party."

"Okay," I said.

She took my pen and wrote down Brian Brain's address, upside down on my notebook. Her handwriting was strange and beautiful.

She got up. "Friday."

"Okay," I said.

# 27

Brian Brain's party was at his parents' house on the east side. I thought he might be poor, but his parents had a big two-story house with a back yard. It was more in the city than where I lived but it was still pretty nice.

I parked down the street. I didn't have Kirk to come with me. I had never socialized with downtown people without him. And I was wearing a buttoned-down shirt, which was too normal, too conservative. But it was too late now.

I went inside. It wasn't that wild. As far as I could tell it was about thirty people from Learning Center (the alternative high school), a few people from Agenda, a few other people from Portland Episcopal and Bradley Day School which were both private. Needless to say, no one from Evergreen was there. At first I didn't see anyone I knew, but then I saw Danielle, Eleanor's friend. She smiled at me in her flirty way. So I talked to her. It was hard though. She was older, twenty-two someone told me, and kind of weird. Like she would kind of blank out in the middle of whatever you were saying. And not look at you. But then a minute later she was being all flirty again.

Danielle was drinking wine. Someone handed me a beer. People were smoking pot; you could smell it. We stood in the kitchen and listened to a guy tell a long story about a rapper who was gay but had sex with all these models and famous actresses so that people wouldn't find out. Everyone laughed at that.

Downstairs was more relaxed. Brian Brain was sitting on a couch with his arms around two girls I didn't know. One of the girls had this really outrageous hairdo and deep eye mascara and they were both wearing skirts so short you could totally see their underwear. The three of them were giggling and sort of laughing at everyone.

That's when I felt a hand on my elbow. It was Eleanor.

"Max," she said. "So nice of you to come."

"So nice of you to have me."

We smiled at each other. I loved how formal she was. I loved how it separated her from other people.

"I was going upstairs to dance," she said, grinning. "Come join me. Won't you?"

"I don't really like to dance," I said.

"Oh but you will," she said. "You will."

# 28

I went with Eleanor. The living room was the dancing room. It was dark and someone had just put on "Brick House." Eleanor led me forward. She held my hands as we started. It seemed like she was finding any excuse to touch me. Every time I looked up she was smiling into my face.

We danced. I did the two-step, back-forth thing that everyone does. Eleanor was a great dancer. You could tell she was toning it down to my level, but even then she was totally sexy and cool. Her hair hung down in her face a bit and her neck was long and she moved with so much . . . personality, I guess. Like everything she did was so expressive, just moving with the music her body was saying, *Life is good but nothing matters.* Or, *I know I'm beautiful but that won't save me from the world.*

There was generosity there too. She liked me and she was letting me know. Maybe not in a romantic way, but in some way. She was honoring me.

We danced. More people came and joined in, and pretty soon the living room was the hot spot of the party. Eleanor obviously knew a lot of the other people, but she never left me. And if other guys wanted to dance with us she would allow it, but she never separated from me. She was mine. At least for tonight.

Finally, she yelled in my ear that she was going downstairs to see how Brian Brain was doing. I felt almost relieved. She left, and I flopped on the couch. I could tell people were looking at me and wondering who I was that Eleanor liked me so much. Then I went to the kitchen and got something to drink. I ended up talking to Danielle and some other girls. I felt very loose and confident now. I could talk to anyone.

Before I left, I went downstairs to find Eleanor and say good-bye. She was on the couch, talking to Brian Brain. I told her I was going, and she wanted to walk me out.

"I'm really glad you came," she said when we were outside. It was a beautiful summer night. The air smelled like sprinklers and grass. The moon was just over the hills above the city.

"I had the best time," I said.

"I'm glad."

"You're so much fun to hang out with."

"I try."

"I wish Kirk wasn't so in love with you," I said. "I would ask you out."

"Would you?" she said, smiling.

I unlocked my car door. I wanted to kiss her. I didn't know how to do it exactly, but I had to try. I stepped forward and kissed the side of her face, lingering for a moment to feel the softness of her cheek.

I stepped back and opened my door.

"That's it?" she said.

"What?"

"That's all the kiss I get?"

I swallowed. I shut the door and approached her again. I touched both her arms and kissed her lips. Her eyes closed as I did it. She smelled different from any girl I'd ever been close to. It was a complicated smell: cigarettes and perfume and downtown cafés. I stopped kissing her and hugged her. She was not a hugging type person. But that's how I felt, so I did it anyway.

"You're such a gentleman," she said, into the side of my head.

"I know," I said.

She pulled away from me and skipped back across the street. I watched her go. She was the coolest girl I had ever known. But I was not in love with her.

Kirk was in love with her.

# 29 - - - - - - - - - - - - - - -

My parents made me take Drea to the Woodridge Mall to get school clothes. She had talked them into giving her one of those kids' credit cards where they put some money on a card and you can use it until it runs out. Drea had three hundred dollars for school clothes. Which wasn't very much.

As we drove she was asking me about Evergreen and being a freshmen. I did my best to tell her. But it wasn't that hard being a freshman. About clothes or girl stuff I didn't know anything. Drea knew better than I did.

"What if I see Cindy?" she said, as we steered through the mall entrance.

"What about it?"

"It'll be so sad."

"No it won't."

"Are you guys even friends?"

"Sure," I said. "I mean, we don't see each other. We will this year. We'll be in the same wing."

"Could you ever get back together with her?"

I pulled up in front of Nordstrom. "I don't know. I guess anything's possible."


That night, I was in the kitchen reading a copy of Portland Episcopal's school paper from last year. Ashley had met me for coffee and given me a whole stack. I was looking for ideas to steal.

The phone rang and Drea yelled for me to pick it up.

"Hello?" I said.

"Max?" said the voice. "It's me, Lydia."

A chill went through me. "Hi Lydia," I said.

"What are you doing?"

"Nothing."

"How is your summer going?"

"Fine."

"Do you hate me?" she asked.

"No Lydia, I don't hate you. What do you want?"

"I want to ask you something."

"What," I said.

"I wanted to ask you if I could work on the paper next year."

"You have to sign up."

"But Dominique said you needed people."

"We do, but you have to sign up."

"But a lot of people work on it who didn't sign up. I thought that was only if you wanted credit."

She was right. I continued to flip through Ashley's school paper.

"Couldn't I write something?" asked Lydia.

"What do you want to write?"

"Dominique said you needed social stuff. Or a column. I could do that. I read all the magazines. I read *YM* and *Cosmo* and *Jane*."

"We need a *regular* column. Weekly. Not just an article now and then."

"I could do that."

"No, you can't."

"Why not."

"You're a sophomore."

"So?"

"And you're not signed up."

"You just don't want me on the paper," she said.

"That's right, I don't."

"You're embarrassed because we hooked up at Dominique's."

"We did not *hook up*."

"What was it then, a *continuation*?"

"It was you pulling one of your little stunts. And thanks a lot for having your mom call my mom."

"That was not my fault."

"Then whose fault was it?"

She paused. "I'm sorry. I thought you liked me. You did kiss me."

"You tricked me into kissing you."

She didn't say anything then. Her silence was very effective. I started to feel bad.

"Listen," I said. "You're not signed up and I honestly don't think you're qualified."

"But I am. I can do it. You know I can."

# 30

August was going by fast. You could feel fall coming. The air had that burnt smell. There was a chill when the sun went down.

Bryce and I went to football practice. We sat in the stands and watched the players. Bryce told me about the cross-country team and a new guy, Nathan Reimer, who was a junior. He had a foot injury last year and hadn't run but this year he was setting records in practice. He was the fastest person who had ever gone to Evergreen, which wasn't that hard since Evergreen had only existed five years.

"So write something about it," I told him. "Get some pictures."

We had our first *Owl* meeting. School wasn't open yet, so we had to stand outside the *Owl* office until Mr. Owens got there. There were about twelve of us. Kirk wasn't back yet but Bryce was there, Jill St. John, Maria Sanchez, Rebecca, "scientific" Kevin, Josh Markowitz who was going to be our photographer, a new round-faced punk girl named Becky Cetera, a couple others.

Then Lydia Kresch showed up. Mr. Owens still hadn't come yet. I frowned at her and she avoided me. When Mr. Owens came she went right to him and asked if she could do stuff for the paper, even though she wasn't signed up.

"Of course," he said.

We went in. We sat. We talked about our first issue. It would be mostly sports, which was normal for the first issue. Bryce had a big piece about Nathan Reimer, the cross-country runner. We had football and girls' soccer, which Maria Sanchez was going to do. We'd have record reviews from Kirk. There was a Jimmy Eat World concert that week; we'd cover that. Jill had some new information about the corrupt food company that supplied our cafeteria.

Then I told everyone that I was worried that we didn't have enough human interest stuff. We didn't have any columns or anything about the social side of school.

Lydia raised her hand.

I was running the meeting at this point. I tried to pretend I didn't see Lydia. But Mr. Owens motioned his head for me to call on her.

"Yes, Lydia," I said.

"I want to do a column."

"Yeah? What about?"

"I don't know yet. But I already wrote one. Do you want to see it?"

"Well . . . "

"Should I read it?"

"Now?"

"Yeah."

I looked at Mr. Owens. But he was watching Lydia. Everyone was. They were wondering who she was, who would dare walk in and assign herself a column.

She stood up. She unfolded a piece of paper. She said her column was called "The New Rules of High School" and this was her first installment.

She started reading. It was short. It was a mess. It was about guys and how they won't ask you out. They never want to commit to anything definite. They only want to meet you places. And if they do call you on your cell phone, they catch you in the most embarrassing places. Like in the bathroom taking a pee. Or when you're at Target trying on bras. It was also about what bad eaters boys are. Like if you go out with them, they take you to Wendy's and then eat with their mouths open.

I thought it was terrible. It was badly written. It wasn't informative. It had no point.

Everyone else loved it. They laughed the whole time she was reading. They clapped when she was done. She did a little bow and sat down.

After the meeting, everyone was buzzing about Lydia's piece. Rebecca and another girl wouldn't shut up about their brothers and how badly they ate.

On his way out, Mr. Owens, put his hand on my shoulder. "Looks like you've got a columnist."

Part Three **Fall**

## 31

School started on a wet gray day in early September. My mom made us breakfast and was trying to act excited for Drea but it felt a little forced. I think Drea just wanted to get there and get it over with.

At school people were surprised to see me driving a car. Peter Daley waved as I pulled into the parking lot. Somebody yelled out, "The Maxmobile!" I saw Cindy's red Ford Explorer by the gym. I parked away from it.

I walked Drea to orientation and then went to the junior/ senior wing. I found my new locker and looked around to see where everyone was. Kirk's locker was near mine on the left. Bob's and Peter's lockers were around the corner. That's where Cindy was. Tara was closer; she was down and across from me. Dominique Taylor and Gabby were next to each other a few lockers in the other direction. It was exciting. It was the new world order.

I had a sudden urge to talk to Cindy. It wouldn't be that awkward; seniors were supposed to welcome juniors into the wing. I walked down and turned the corner, and there she was. She was tan and blonder than usual. She was wearing jeans and a white shirt. Her face looked different. She looked older.

"Hey," I said, coming up beside her.

"Oh!" she said, startled. She immediately averted her eyes. "Hi Max."

"Didn't mean to scare you," I said. "I just wanted to welcome you to the junior/senior wing."

"Thanks," she said. She did something with her locker door. "I think my locker's broken," she said.

I looked at it. One of the hinges was broken.

"You're right," I said, moving the door back and forth. "You should get them to fix this."

"Who do you report it to?"

"The main office."

This was the first conversation we'd had since I saw her at the mall two months ago.

"How are things going?" I asked. But I was losing my air of casual confidence. My heart was starting to race.

"Okay," she said, tightly. "How was your summer?"

"Okay."

"I better go tell them about this," she said.

"Yeah, they'll fix it for you."

Fourth period I went to the *Owl*. The first issue was done and would come out on Wednesday. The front page was the big football preview. I had made Bryce put his cross-country piece in the back. In the Student Life section was a back-to-school article, a fall calendar, some practical info, a map for the freshmen.

It would also have Lydia Kresch's first column in it, as well as my first editorial, which I had worried about for weeks and which wasn't very good. It was about how Evergreen is our own creation and it was our responsibility to make it fun and not a chore to come every day. When Rebecca gave it the headline "Supporting School Spirit" I instantly knew how bad it was.

To make matters worse, on Tuesday Nathan Reimer beat the reigning cross-country state champion by half a mile. Everyone was talking about it, which was weird because even if he was really good, it was still only cross-country. Who cared about that? But then I saw him in the cafeteria and realized why everyone was into him. He looked like Jesus Christ. Seriously. He had long wavy dark hair, a tan handsome face, big white teeth. He dressed sort of hippie cool, with a necklace and leather things around his wrists. In the cafeteria all these people were talking to him, congratulating him, girls especially. He was a total star. And I had buried him in the back of the paper.

The *Owl* came out. The first issue appeared in the usual stacks, like last year, in certain rooms, in the cafeteria, in the library. Even though my editorial sucked it was still thrilling to see it. Everywhere I went, I looked to see if people were reading it. I would ask people what they thought. Nobody thought much. It was just the paper. Drea said the map was pointless because they gave you a much better one at orientation.

The only thing that seemed to have an impact was Lydia's column. Guys were complaining about it. Girls were reading it in little packs. At the cafeteria, every girl was reading page five, which was where Lydia's column was.

Kirk and I stayed late after school that day. We read through the whole paper. I was sitting at Mr. Owens' desk, my feet up on the desktop.

"What do you think?" I asked.

"Lydia's thing is the best."

"I know. What about the rest?"

"It sucks," he said.

"Yeah," I said.

"Even my review sucks."

"CD reviews are boring."

"What do we do?" he asked.

"I don't know."

"Make it funnier."

"Get Mr. All-American Cross-Country Guy on the front page," I said, tossing the paper on my desk and putting my feet down. Kirk was still reading. I watched him. I had been thinking I should tell him about my night with Eleanor. But so far I couldn't.

## 32

Lydia's second installment of "The New Rules of High School" was about "plexing," which was sneaking into different movies at the cineplex besides the one you paid for. It was also about how boys like the stupidest movies and go see them over and over. And how all the actresses now have implants to enhance their breasts and why can't guys get implants to enhance their brains. It was a big hit. It was all anyone talked about. So far, Lydia was carrying the paper.

Her third column was about Nathan Reimer. It was called "The Hot Jock." It was a list of the reasons Nathan was a "hottie," the reasons he was a "biscuit," the reasons he was a total "spaniel." I didn't know girls were calling guys "spaniels," or even what that meant. But that didn't matter.

"We can't run this," I told Lydia, when I'd finished it. "This is a personals ad."

"It's a column."

"No, it's not."

Lydia stood over me. She had come to the *Owl* office to show it to me. She was suddenly hanging out there a lot.

"I think it's fine. I think people will like it."

"It's not appropriate. It puts Nathan on the spot. We can't have people writing love letters to individual people in the school paper."

"You're jealous," she said. "You're jealous and you don't like me writing a column anyway."

"I'm not jealous. What would I be jealous of?"

"Nathan."

"I'm happy for Nathan. He's bringing honor to us all."

"You're jealous that I like him now. And not you."

This was an interesting statement. I wondered if it could be true.

"And you're jealous that people like my column." She snatched the paper from me. "I'm going to ask Mr. Owens."

That night, Lydia called me at home. "I'm sorry I said you were jealous," she said.

"It's all right," I said. "What did Mr. Owens say?"

"He agreed with you. Of course. Nathan *is* a total hottie though."

"I know. The girls are all over him in the cafeteria."

"Where did he come from? Nobody knew him last year."

"He was injured. Something with his foot."

"It's weird how people become popular all of a sudden," she said.

"When I broke up with Cindy, I was so sure she was about to become super popular."

"Did she?"

"No. She kept being Cindy."

"What's she doing these days?"

"I don't know," I said. "I never really see her."

"But you guys must talk."

"She doesn't seem to want to."

"She probably still likes you."

"I doubt that."

I could hear her moving around in her room. The radio was on behind her. "Wait, so why can't we run my piece about Nathan again?" she asked.

"You can't do stuff like that in a school paper."

"You sound like a teacher."

"In a way, I am."


The next morning I talked to Jill St. John in the parking lot. She was working with a new anarchist environmental group called Anarcadia. They were spiking trees in British Columbia. She was going to write about it. It was illegal of course, but it sounded cool, and I told her we could find a way to cover it in the *Owl*.

"What can you do for pictures?" I asked.

"Can we do pictures?"

"Sure, we can do anything," I said, feeling the power of my position.

"I don't have a good camera."

"Talk to Josh Markowitz."

"I will. That's a good idea. Thanks."

I told her good luck. I walked to class.


That night Lydia called again.

"What are you doing?" she said.

"Nothing. Rewriting my college essay."

"Do you mind that I call you?"

"No. I'm actually getting sick of this. It's about my deaf uncle. And how he overcomes his obstacles."

"Yuck."

"I know," I said.

"I could read it over for you if you want. If that would help."

"Nah, that's all right."

"Would you mind if I ask you something?"

"What?"

"Are you glad I'm on the paper?"

I sighed.

"You have to admit I'm turning into a good columnist."

"I would have to admit that. Yes."

"But you still don't like it. You don't like girls who are smart."

"That's not true."

"But you never trust me about things. Like I knew I could do the column. Just like I knew that you and I would . . . you know . . . "

"What?"

"We would be friends. I totally knew it. But you always act like I'm impossible."

"You *are* impossible. The first time I met you, you were cheating at spin-the-bottle. What kind of person cheats at spin-the-bottle?"

"A smart person?"

I thought about it. "Well, maybe so."

"And it worked out didn't it? And we are becoming friends aren't we? At least a little bit?"

"All I'm saying is your personal style is a little . . . Some people don't like to be steamrolled into things, okay?"

"I promise I won't try to *steamroll* you into things."

"Yeah, like that will last."


That weekend my mom wanted to start doing my college applications. For real. I took a shower and put on a clean shirt. We went into the living room and started laying them all out on the dining room table. It was an impressive sight. Harvard, Yale, Stanford, Brown, UC Berkeley, Princeton, Northwestern. Drea came in and watched us. It was hard having her there. She wasn't going to get this treatment.

On Monday driving to school, I asked her how school was going.

"It's hard to meet people."

"Yeah."

"When I say my last name they say, 'Are you Max's little sister?'"

"Is that bad?"

"Are you kidding? It's horrible."

"Oh," I said. "I didn't know. I'm sorry."

# 33

The first party of that year was at Gabby Greenberg's house. It wasn't supposed to be super big, but first parties tended to get that way. Everyone wanted to see everyone else. They wanted to see who people's new friends were.

Dominique Taylor was there. And Bryce. And Charlton Hughes. Nathan Reimer was there. And Lydia Kresch and Jane and some of their gang; they were all sophomores now. Freshman babe Sonya Taylor was there with another super-cute freshman girl that everyone was suddenly talking about. Roberta Handel was her name. People were talking about her so much that Kirk and I had actually gone to the frosh/soph wing one day to try to figure out who she was. But we couldn't find her. The word was, she was even hotter than Sonya, who was hotter than Dominique, who had been the hottest girl at Evergreen for the last two years. So you can imagine how curious people were.

Gabby's house was huge. Kirk and I walked around the grounds. Kirk was in a weird mood. It was probably something about visiting his dad in Minneapolis. There was bad history there.

The party helped. People were everywhere, on the deck, in the yard, in every room. There was music in the basement. People were dancing. Lydia found me and asked me to dance. I didn't want to, but I did anyway. I was more of a public person now that I was running the *Owl*. It was important that I look like I was having a good time.

There were a lot of people dancing. Peter Daley waved to me and then gestured toward a girl in a tight white top. Everyone was watching her. It was Roberta Handel. She was tiny. And she had this strange smile that looked painted on. She looked like a little doll. I tried not to stare, but it was hard, she was so plastic looking. Still, there she was: the freshman girl everyone was talking about. There was one every year.


Lydia eventually spotted Nathan and ran off to talk to him. Kirk and I went upstairs. A bunch of new people had come while we were dancing. People from other schools. Ashley Cole appeared. She talked to me briefly, but in her usual distracted way. She said she had applied early decision to Barnard.

And then Eleanor walked in. That was a shock. And Brian Brain too. He was dressed in an outrageous white preppy sweater, white slacks, and white Nikes—with black eyeliner. He saw Kirk and me and came over and did high-fives and said, "Whasssssupp?" in a mocking voice, making fun of our stupid high school party.

"What are you doing here?" I said.

Brian Brain shrugged and said Kirk had invited them.

I avoided Eleanor, with Kirk there. Thankfully, Kirk grabbed her and led her onto the deck where the beer was. That left me and Brian Brain standing in Gabby Greenberg's living room. Brian Brain dug his cigarettes out of his pocket. He lit one.

"I don't think they want you to smoke here," said some-one, as politely as they could. Brian Brain was looking a little scary.

"Oh, pardon me," he answered. He dropped his lit ciga-rette on the carpet and smashed it in with his toe. It left a black burn mark in the carpet.


I got away from him. I took the back stairs to the basement.

Cindy was there by the stairs. With Tara. Bryce was talking to Cindy.

I didn't like that. I went to the other side of the room. I grabbed a Coke out of the downstairs fridge and sat on a couch in the corner. Tara saw me and came over to say hi. She said she liked the paper this year. She liked Lydia's columns.

"Yeah," I said. "Everybody likes her stuff."

Cindy finished her conversation with Charlton and reluc-tantly came over. Tara sat on the couch beside me. Cindy sat on the arm of the couch, away from me, next to Tara.

"How is your year going so far?" I asked Tara.

"Okay," she said. The three of us sat there. Cindy wouldn't look at me, but at least she was there. At least we weren't hiding from each other. Then Tara got up. She asked if we wanted something. Cindy wanted a Coke.

"Save my seat," Tara said as she left. She pointed for Cindy to sit next to me. Cindy acted like she didn't under-stand. But then Tara grabbed her and pushed her down on the couch beside me.

## 34

I wasn't prepared for Cindy to land in my lap. She wasn't either. We both scooted away from each other.

We didn't talk. We watched the dancing. The music had changed though, and people were mostly standing around.

"See that girl?" I said, pointing into the crowd. "That's Roberta Handel."

"Who's she?" said Cindy.

"She's the new freshman girl that everyone talks about."

"Really?"

I nodded. "She's kind of weird looking," I said.

"She looks like a doll."

"That's what I thought."

Cindy watched her. "Do you like her?" she asked.

"No," I said.

Cindy was still shifting, still moving herself away from me slightly. I could smell her though. It was a familiar smell, a wonderful smell. It made my brain race and my throat go dry. Then I wanted to touch her, to hold her hand or put my arm around her.

"How's school?" I said.

She shrugged. "Okay."

I nodded.

"How's the paper?" she asked.

"Not as good as it could be."

"You say that about everything."

"No, I don't."

"You don't think anything's good enough."

I didn't answer.

Tara came back. "Jeez, you guys, try not to look so miserable," she said.

Cindy got up. "I have to go," she said to Tara. She went upstairs.

I walked around. I looked for Kirk. I was a little worried about him.

He was in the back yard with Jimmy Simpson, Evergreen's foremost pot-head. I didn't see Eleanor. Brian Brain didn't appear to be around either.

"Hey," I said to Kirk.

He didn't respond. He had a big plastic cup of keg beer he was drinking from. He and Jimmy and some other guys were smoking a joint.

Kirk took a hit off it.

"Did Eleanor take off?" I asked.

He didn't answer. He handed the joint to Jimmy. I decided to leave him alone. I walked back to the house.

I went upstairs. Roberta Handel was in the kitchen with Sonya Taylor. Charlton Hughes was there too, hitting on Roberta it looked like. He'd probably get her, too. Nathan Reimer was talking to another girl who was so thrilled, she looked like she was going to faint.

Lydia and Jane were there. Peter Daley was there. Sonya Taylor was getting something out of the fridge. She was sticking her head deep into it. I leaned over the door and watched her. It was weird that she was my sister's age. I couldn't imagine Drea at a party like this.

Then Bob Hollins rushed into the room. He grabbed Peter and me and said that Kirk had gotten in a fight in the back with a guy from Portland Episcopal. We all ran down the stairs and into the yard.

But whatever had happened was over. Kirk was gone. The other guy was standing with his friends. He was touching his bloody lip and telling people Kirk sucker punched him. A couple of his buddies were already looking for Kirk.

I snuck off. I knew where Kirk's car was parked. I ran around the house and down the street.

Kirk was there, in his car. The door was open. He was sitting sideways in the driver's seat, his feet on the curb, drinking the rest of his beer.

"Kirk, hey, what happened?"

He didn't answer. He looked away from me.

I waited a second to catch my breath. I glanced back toward the house. Fortunately, no one had followed me. "Are you all right?" I said.

Kirk glared up at me. "Why didn't you tell me about you and Eleanor?"

"I . . . I didn't think there was anything to tell."

"She said you guys hung out after I left."

"We went to a party, in August. I ran into her."

He stared at his dashboard.

"We ..." I continued. "Nothing really happened. It didn't seem that important—"

"She said you're a good kisser."

I tried to think of a reply. "She kissed me good night and it got a little . . . you know how she is."

"You're not a very loyal person are you?"

"I didn't think it would matter. I mean—"

"You dumped Cindy for no reason," he said. "And you didn't tell me about Dominique's pool party. And now you're fooling around with the only girl I ever liked."

"You know how she is—"

"The ONLY GIRL!" he shouted.

I nodded. "Yeah," I said. "I know. I'm sorry. But she's the one who did it. She's the one who isn't loyal."

"Of course she's not! She's not supposed to be. *You're* supposed to be. You're supposed to be my friend."

"I'm sorry," I said. "I wanted to say something about it. I didn't know how."

Kirk threw his beer cup into the neighbor's lawn and swung his legs into his car.

"Kirk, don't leave yet."

He started the car.

"Dude, you're wasted. Let me—"

He turned on the headlights and pulled away from the curb.

I ran along the car for a few steps. "Kirk, hey!"

But there was no stopping him. He was gone.

## 35

I got a ride home from the party with Dominique Taylor and her sister Sonya and three freshmen girls. We were all in Dominique's SUV. I was sitting in the very back. The three freshmen were bunched forward, chattering away.

"Oh my god, did you see Nathan talking to that stupid Glencoe girl?"

"There's no way he can go with a girl from there."

"Farm girls—"

"Totally—"

"Sluts—"

"Who does Nathan like?"

"Roberta."

"Who *everybody* likes."

"What's so great about her?"

"Did you see her?"

"What's up with her pants?"

"Her ass is like a boy's."

"Lydia Kresch was chasing Nathan."

"If *she* gets him—"

"She'll probably have sex with him."

"I'd have sex with him."

"I'd have sex with him."

"No, you wouldn't."

"Yes, I would."

"I might have sex with him, if he asked me nicely."

"What about Charlton Hughes?"

"*Oh . . . my . . . god.*"

"Sleaze."

"Hottie though."

"Don't go in his sauna."

"I'll go in his sauna."

"Ho!"

"You're a ho!"

"I bet if you asked Nathan he'd go out with you."

"He would."

"Yeah but who's going to ask him?"

"Me."

"Me."

"No, *not you.*"

"I heard he did it with an eighth grader."

"No way!"

"Nathan did?"

"Yeah, but when he was a freshman."

"Cross-country runners can't have sex before a race."

"That's a myth."

"They *have* to have sex, it releases their whattayacallit."

"Testosterone."

"His lips look like a girl's. But in a good way."

"I love his whiskers."

"He looks like Tobey Maguire."

"*Oh . . . my . . . god!*"

"Tobey Maguire."

"Totally Tobey."

"Tobey Maguire is like, *the* most—"

"I bet Roberta gets Nathan."

"Somebody has to ask him out!"

"I saw him talking to Cindy Sherman."

"Tonight?"

"I did too."

"Really? Cindy?"

"Shhhhhh, Max is in the car."

"Oh God, Max Caldwell is in the car."

"Shhhhhh."

Giggles.

"He can't hear, he's in the back."

"He's asleep."

"Kirk got in a fight."

"Who's Kirk?"

"Max's friend. That punk guy."

"Cindy and Charlton, that's what I heard. Last summer."

"What happened?"

"Shhhh."

"Don't talk about her."

"Was Nathan dancing?"

"Yes."

"With Roberta."

"Who does Roberta like?"

"She's so conceited, have you noticed?"

"Do you think?"

"I like Roberta."

"I like Roberta."

"No, I like Roberta, I'm saying she seems conceited *at first*."

"You have to get to know her."

"Her hair is weird."

"Her hair *is* weird."

"That haircut cost two hundred dollars."

"Gabby Greenberg's mom gets clothes free from Nordstrom."

"But only ski parkas and sports bras."

"What else about Nathan?"

"Who did he dance with?"

"Cindy."

"Shhhh. . . . "

"Max doesn't care."

"Guys love Cindy. She's so soft."

"Her breasts got bigger."

"Shhhhh."

"Max broke up with her. It's his own fault."

"Who's Max go out with?"

"I bet Nathan will end up with Roberta."

"Oh my god."

"Nathan."

"Nathan Reimer is like, *the* most—"

"My dream boy."

"Oh Nathan, *kiss me*!"

"Shut up!"

"Stop it!"

"You're so gay!"

- - -

Dominique dropped the freshmen off first. Once they were gone, the car got very quiet. I moved up to the middle seat. Dominique asked me something about the paper and I answered, but then the car fell silent again.

- - - - - - - - - - - - - - - **36**

Kirk survived his drive home that night. At least I didn't hear any tragic news on Monday. Mostly what I heard was more talk about the party. People were laughing, gossiping in the halls: Nathan, Roberta, who was with who.

I found Kirk in the cafeteria at lunch. I sat with him. He didn't say anything. I didn't either. I offered him my cupcake. He shook his head.

That night Lydia called me at home.

"I heard you were talking to Nathan," I said.

"As a matter of fact I was."

"Did you tell him you wrote a column about him? And that your cruel editor wouldn't let you print it?"

"Actually, I did."

"And what did he say?"

"He wanted to read it."

"Did you let him?"

"We have a date on Friday," said Lydia. "I might let him read it then."

"Wait. *You're* going out with Nathan?"

"Don't be jealous. You had your chance. And you rejected me."

"No way are you going out with him," I said. "He likes Roberta. They're the hot new couple. I heard it from a bunch of freshmen girls."

"*Freshmen girls*," scoffed Lydia. "Like they know anything."

That week we sent off my college applications. My mom and I did most of it, but my dad was helping too. Drea watched TV. She watched a lot more TV since she started high school. She would lie there on the floor with her homework all day after school. She had originally planned to go out for soccer. But she didn't do it for some reason. My parents were starting to worry about her.

At the *Owl*, we had delayed putting Nathan on the cover until he ran against the state champion guy again. That day was now approaching. So it was time for our big Nathan Reimer issue. Bryce was writing the article. Josh Markowitz would take the pictures. The day of the meet, a bunch of us drove out to the park where they ran the race.

Lydia came. She had been on her date with Nathan, but I couldn't tell what had happened. It couldn't have gone that well, if she wouldn't tell me about it.

None of us had actually seen a cross-country event before. The starting line was in the woods, at the head of a hiking trail. It was pretty rugged terrain. And muddy. But it was October now, and the trees were all turning colors, and the air was crisp and cold, so that was cool.

There was also press there. Like real adult journalists from real newspapers, with real photographers. They were all talking about Nathan. When it was time, a guy stood in front of the racers with a starting gun. Everyone got excited. Lydia especially. She actually yelled out, "Go Nathan!" It kind of bugged me.

The guy shot the gun. The racers ran into the woods. They were like deer, the way they took off, fast-moving but perfectly quiet. But what happened then? Were we supposed to stand there for an hour until they came back? Cross-country wasn't much of a spectator sport.

# 37

Nathan won the race easily. Josh got a slightly blurry but usable shot of him coming across the finish line, arms raised, huge smile, etc. We ran it on the cover that week. A half-page picture, which was the biggest the printer would let us do. People loved it. In the same issue Lydia had a column about how to make boys like you in ten seconds or less, and everyone loved that too. It was a one-two punch. The papers were gone from their stacks in two hours. Usually it took two days.

Also, by this time, people had begun to talk about Nathan and Lydia. But people seemed oddly unexcited about it. The attitude was like, "Oh, I guess Lydia and Nathan are hanging out." Lydia was doing her best to legitimize it though. Her next column was about having a jock for a boyfriend. How you had to adjust to their schedule. You couldn't do "certain things" on certain days, because it "diminished their energy." You had to attend their events and cheer, even though you didn't know the rules or what exactly was happening.

There was something not right about it, though. Lydia was trying too hard. I could feel it. One day we snuck off campus to McDonald's. I tried to hint to her that she shouldn't get too hopeful about Nathan. Sure she was popular now too, with her column, but he was on a different level of popularity. He was on Roberta's level, the mindless beautiful people level. That was the highest level. You couldn't break into it by *doing* something. You had to already *be* something.

She wasn't buying it, though. She wouldn't really listen to anything I said.

Drea was having social problems too. She almost cried one morning when I pulled in front of the frosh/soph wing. She said she felt so tired when she walked in there. It was like they sucked the air out of her. She said she tried to borrow a chair from Sonya Taylor's table one day in the cafeteria and a girl grabbed it out of her hand and then everyone laughed at her.

"I didn't know it was taken," said Drea. "How was I supposed to know?"

"I felt the same way about Dominique when she first came."

"It's not like I'm trying to be friends with them. I'm just trying to exist. What do they care?"

I thought for a second. "Why don't you come by the paper later?" I said.

"Why?"

"Maybe you could do something."

"Like what?"

"Help with sports. Or maybe do something with photography. Josh always needs people."

"Oh God, the assistant to the school paper photographer?"

"Hey, it's something. You gotta start somewhere."

That afternoon Peter Daley and I saw a group of people gathered around Charlton Hughes's BMW. We went over to see what was up.

He was playing the new White Stripes CD. The White Stripes were a band that only had two people in it, a guy and his sister. Charlton was telling everyone that the guy had sex with his sister. He knew it for sure because his cousin worked for a record company in L.A. Charlton claimed that everyone in the music industry knew about it, but they kept it out of the press. People were saying it couldn't be true, but Charlton was into it. He really liked the idea of the brother/sister sex thing.

I left them all arguing and went to my car. I wished Kirk was around but he was still pissed at me. Two weekends had

gone by and we had barely spoken. He was probably hanging out downtown with Brian Brain and those people. The
club kids, Lydia called them. She had met Eleanor and
Brian Brain at the big party. She loved them of course. She
decided Eleanor was her idol.

Kirk's silent treatment was also hurting the paper. He
had written one article in three weeks. Becky Cetera was
writing most of the music reviews now. I never actually
talked to her. Becky and Kirk seemed to be working it out
between them.

Finally, one day, I caught Kirk at his locker. He tried to walk
away but I wouldn't let him. "Listen," I said, "I know you
think I let you down. But this isn't about that. This is the
paper."

"Who cares about the paper. The paper sucks."

"The paper is what we do. If the paper sucks, that means
*we* suck."

"We do suck," he said. "*You* suck especially. You dissed
Lydia so hard. You wouldn't even talk to her. Now you're best
friends since everybody likes her stupid column."

"We're not best friends."

"You'd sell out anyone for the stupid paper. So you can
go to stupid Harvard."

It took me a second to absorb that insult. There was
some truth in it.

"Listen, can you just try to think of something new for
Student Life?" I said. "We can't have all record reviews. It
sucks, Kirk. You know it does. We need other things."

"Like what?"

"I don't know what . . . like . . . how about something . . . about club kids."

"What club kids?"

"Brian Brain and Eleanor and those guys."

"I'm not putting those people in my high school paper."

"Why not?"

"They'd never agree to it."

But I was picturing it in my mind. It was a great idea. Club kids. "Get Josh Markowitz," I said. "Get Becky Cetera and go downtown and take pictures of people dancing. Get the wildest girls. Get Brian Brain and Eleanor and Danielle."

Kirk thought about it. He began to see what I saw: clueless Evergreen students looking at pictures of Brian Brain in makeup. Or even reading the name "Brian Brain." He saw AP geeks gawking at pictures of super-hot girls in miniskirts on the dance floor at Agenda. People would freak. It would totally mess with their heads.

"Huh," said Kirk. "Maybe that would be cool."

This was why Kirk was my best friend.

- - - - - - - - - - - - - - - - **38**

So that's how the year was going. Drama, crises, politics. It was fun in a way. It was definitely time-consuming.

Meanwhile, all around me, people were hooking up. Everywhere I went someone was talking about a date they were on. Even really plain guys were suddenly talking to girls in the parking lot, or meeting them at football games or whatever. And it was October, so the weather was perfect and there were dances and parties and new movies to go to. I guess it was because we were seniors now. There was almost a sense of obligation. This was our last year together, it would be rude or antisocial to not ask someone out.

I, on the other hand, did nothing but work. It was good, because I felt like every issue of the *Owl* was better than the last one. Also, the fast pace of it worked perfectly for me. Talk about "racing brain," I was in that mode all the time. It made me realize the reason my brain used to race before was because I didn't have anything to keep it occupied. Now my brain was full. Now I had stuff to worry about every second. It felt great.

And then there was Cindy. I kept waiting for her to have a boyfriend. But all I ever heard was how withdrawn she was. Even Tara complained about how she never wanted to do anything. It was comforting in a way. I liked the idea that we were both too busy or preoccupied. We'd already been in love. We had other concerns now. And the fact that neither of us had someone, it gave us a connection. I'd be alone, working late at the *Owl*, and I'd think *she's alone somewhere too. . . .*

Kirk did the club kids article. He took Becky Cetera with him and Josh Markowitz. They went to Agenda and took pictures but they weren't that good. Josh was kind of clueless. So we sent them back again. This time Brian Brain took Josh around and made him take better pictures, like shooting people dancing from knee level, "so you get a lot of leg," according to Brian Brain. He also made Josh "get in people's faces," because he always stood too far back. That worked great. Josh got a fish-eye shot of Brian Brain from about six inches from his face. It was hilarious and perfectly captured the shock value aesthetic of the Agenda crowd.

That week we put Brian Brain's picture on the cover and another picture, inside, of a girl, which was practically looking up her skirt. For that same issue Lydia wrote a column about Eleanor and the idea of the femme fatale and how boring Evergreen was and how people needed to have some imagination and live out their fantasies. It was our best issue yet. Every copy was gone in forty-five minutes.


The next day Mr. Owens called me into his office. I thought he was going to tell me how great I was doing, how great the paper was. But he told me not to have any more pictures of girls in short skirts from a low angle.

"You can't see anything," I said.

"It's the principle of it."

"People really like that issue though. Did you see how fast it went out?"

Mr. Owens smiled. He was a weird teacher. Sometimes it seemed like he only came to school to see what amusing trouble his students would get into.

"And everyone loves Lydia," I said, sucking up a bit. "That was a good call Mr. Owens."

"The success of a school paper isn't necessarily measured in how many people read it. Or how fast it goes out," he said. "It's what it stands for. Which is true for a lot of things."

"What do you mean?" I said.

"What does your *Owl* stand for?"

"Just . . . our lives."

"What part of your lives?"

"The fun part?"

Mr. Owens smiled. "I think you're doing a good job," he said. "Just remember that when you work hard at something, your soul gets involved. Even if you don't intend it to."

I nodded. I wasn't sure what he meant exactly. But I was willing to think about it. And I did.

# 39 - - - - - - - - - - - - -

Then one day, on my way home, I saw Cindy and Tara in the parking lot, standing over Tara's car. Her battery had gone dead and the two of them were trying to jump-start it with Cindy's Ford Explorer. They had the hoods up and the jumper cables out. But they weren't sure what to do with them. When they saw me, Tara waved me over.

"Do you know how to do this?" Tara asked.

I looked at the jumper cables and at the two car batteries. The Ford Explorer was running. With the hood open it made a wheezy, airy sound.

"Uhm," I said. I didn't know. I was clueless about cars. "I think it's about positive and negative."

"Obviously," said Cindy. "But what do we do?"

I looked at the jumper cable handles. One was red and one was black. "One of these is red and one is black," I said.

"We know," said Tara. "But what do we do with them?"

I leaned over Tara's battery. It was old and corroded. "I think you put them like this. . . . "

"Whoa, dude, you're going to blow up her car," said Dave Winchell. He had come up behind me. I hadn't heard him with the engine running.

He took the cables. He reversed the black and red handles and attached them. He jumped into Tara's car. We all stood back. He turned the key and it backfired and made some other noises. Then it started.

I helped Dave take the jumper cables off.

"Thanks," said Cindy. Tara drove right off. She was afraid it would die again before she got home.

Dave Winchell disappeared as well. Cindy couldn't reach her hood. I had to pull it down for her. I slammed it shut.

She stood there for a second. Then she got into her car. I stood at her window.

"Thanks, Max," she said.

"No problem," I said.

She sat there. Her engine was already running, so she didn't need to start her car. I think she wanted to talk. I did. But what to say?

"What have you been up to?" I asked.

She shrugged.

"Doing anything fun this weekend?" I asked.

She stared at me. "Are you asking me out?"

"No, no, I . . . I was just asking."

She shifted her car into reverse and backed up. She looked at me once and then drove away.

"Do you think Cindy would go out with me if I asked her on a date?" I asked Drea that night while we watched TV.

"No."

"Why not?"

"Because you already broke her heart."

"We broke each other's hearts. Maybe we can fix it. Or at least we could be friends again."

"You can't be friends again. You can't go backward."

"But maybe she'd just like to go to a movie sometime."

"She probably would. But not with you."

"Do you think Cindy would go out with me if I asked her on a date?" I asked Peter Daley and Bob Hollins in the parking lot the next morning.

"No," said Bob Hollins.

"Why would you do that?" said Peter.

"She hates your guts," said Bob Hollins.

"She doesn't hate my guts," I said.

"Yeah? What happened when you tried to talk to her at Gabby's party?"

"She would barely talk to me," I admitted.

"Do you like her again?" said Peter.

"Kind of. I kind of never stopped liking her."

"Do you think Cindy would go out with me if I asked her on a date?" I asked Kirk in the cafeteria.

"Dude."

"What?"

"Bad idea."

"No, I was just thinking . . . "

"Don't think. Don't ask her out. Do her a favor. Leave her alone."

"Do you think Cindy would go out with me if I asked her on a date?" I asked Lydia one night on the phone.

"Yes," said Lydia. "I think she would, and I think you should ask her. You guys still have stuff to work out."

"We do?"

"Of course. It's obvious."

At the next *Owl* meeting, I brought up the issues Mr. Owens had brought up with me. That we perhaps lacked a social conscience. Kirk got kind of fidgety the minute I said it. He hated stuff with a social conscience. Jill St. John thought we were a bit preoccupied with Nathan Reimer. But she couldn't be too critical, since she had only written two articles for us in the last month. She had been busy with Anarcadia and her new anarchist boyfriend.

"We can't rely on Jill's environmental articles for our morals," said Maria Sanchez. "We all have to contribute."

"But what should we do?" I said.

"The Glencoe paper has this thing called 'Voices'?" said Rebecca, pushing her glasses up her nose. "Where they have different people answering questions about issues that affect the students?"

I saw Kirk roll his eyes. Becky Cetera yawned. They were sitting together. They always sat together lately.

"And they make it an even mix of the different ethnic groups and sexes and all the different grades."

"'Voices,'" I said, thinking about it.

"And they ask them about things like teen pregnancy," said Rebecca. "Or terrorism or whatever's current."

"I think we can guess the kind of questions 'Voices' would require," said Kirk, with great disdain.

"I'm just making a suggestion," said Rebecca.

"Maybe it could work," said Maria Sanchez.

"They have our demographic breakdown on Evergreen's main Web site," said scientific Kevin. He went to one of the computers. "I can run the numbers."

We all sat and waited.

"Male to female," he said. "Is 48 percent to 52 percent. There are . . . 512 freshman . . . 478 sophomores . . . 424 juniors . . . 468 seniors. Ethnic breakdown is . . . African

American 6 percent. Asian American 11 percent. Hispanic American 12 percent. Other . . . "

"What about those new Russian people?" said someone.

"They count as white," said someone else.

"They're weird," said Josh Markowitz.

"What about wiggers?" said Lydia.

"What's a wigger?" said Rebecca, pushing her glasses back up her nose.

"White kids who think they're black," said Kevin, scientifically.

"Really?" said Rebecca. "And they go to our school?"

"You know Jimmy Simpson, people like that," said someone.

"Jimmy Simpson thinks he's black?" said Rebecca.

"I'll do that," announced Lydia. "I'll write a column about it."

- - - - - - - - - - - - - - - - - **40**

Lydia wrote her piece about white kids who think they're black, or rather, who pretend they're black. She never actually used the word "wigger," nor did she mention Jimmy Simpson by name. She did manage to perfectly describe him and his buddies wearing their sideways baseball hats and their Gary Payton jerseys and their fake gold necklaces. And how they let their Fubu pants hang halfway off their asses. Or how they sat around outside the cafeteria harassing freshmen girls, saying "Yo bitch!" and referring to their "cribs" and their "rides" and the "ghe-tto" and otherwise mangling black slang.

I read it. I thought it was funny. Some of the details were dead on. I didn't think we should run it though. I smelled trouble.

Kirk read it. He thought it was the greatest thing he'd ever read.

Maria Sanchez thought it was funny. She was Mexican, so her opinion counted extra. But she also thought it was a little risky. We didn't have any black students on the *Owl* staff, so we couldn't get a true test reading.

Mr. Owens read it. He thought it posed an interesting problem. Can you talk about racial characteristics without being insensitive? Was noting a phenomenon like this, which everyone knew existed, in itself an inappropriate act?

He left it to my discretion.

I didn't want to run it. I had this feeling. But I didn't want to look like I was afraid. Not in front of Lydia. Or Kirk. . . .

We ran it. The issue came out. Sure enough, I was called into Mr. Brown's office at third period. He was freaking out. Mrs. Fourchette, the French teacher, was there. Actually it was she who was freaking out. She was yelling at Mr. Brown. She was kind of uptight in general. Mr. Brown was confused.

But he was taking action. He was confiscating all the papers that were still in the stacks around the school. An announcement had gone over the intercom that the papers were defective and anyone who had taken one was to return it. The clueless freshmen and some sophomores were actually doing it. They were walking around with apologetic looks on their faces, trying to give the papers back.

I sat in Mr. Brown's office while he yelled at the secretaries and other teachers who were carrying the stacks of the *Owl* into his office and piling them against one wall. I had considered this a risk, but I didn't think it would be this bad. What if this went on my transcript somehow? What if my parents found out?

Mr. Owens was brought in. He stuck to his story. He didn't know if it was racist or not. He had deferred to me.

Mrs. Fourchette was furious. Mr. Brown hadn't actually read it. One of the secretaries was reading it. She didn't see what the problem was.

I sat thinking about Lydia. They had sent for her. A lot would depend on how she handled herself.

Lydia arrived. Mr. Brown didn't know who she was. He thought she was one of the clueless freshmen trying to return her paper.

But that changed fast. "What?" demanded Lydia, when she saw the looks of anguish on everyone's faces.

"You wrote this?" said Mr. Brown.

"Yeah, what's wrong with it?" said Lydia. This wasn't the

approach I would have taken. But I waited to see how it would play out.

Mr. Brown wasn't exactly sure what was wrong with it. He looked at Mrs. Fourchette.

"This is the worst example of racism and insensitivity," said Mrs. Fourchette.

Lydia stared at her. "Why?"

"Because . . . " said Mrs. Fourchette. "You're stereotyping . . ."

"Who am I stereotyping?"

"You can't talk about black students . . . " said Mr. Brown.

"I'm not talking about black students. I'm talking about white students," said Lydia with a look of contempt that shut everyone up.

Right then a black girl, one of the few at our school, was walking by the office, laughing into the paper.

"Either way," said Mr. Brown, timidly, "this is going to cause trouble."

I bit my thumbnail. This was getting interesting.

"We ran it by some of the students in the *Owl* office," said Mr. Owens. "Nobody was offended."

"What about the black students?" asked one of the secretaries.

"They love it," said Lydia. "They don't think we write enough about them as it is."

"Can you print . . . *'yo bitch'* in a school newspaper?" Mr. Brown asked Mr. Owens.

No one knew.

Mrs. Fourchette didn't think so. But she had lost her momentum.

"All right, but we're going to hold the papers," said Mr. Brown. "And I don't want any more of this kind of thing in the future. Do you hear me?"

Lydia didn't answer.

"Yes sir," I said.


And thus the great wiggers disaster was averted. No parents complained. But then, only a fraction of the papers made it out.

And of course Lydia's wiggers column became an underground phenomenon. The people who had gotten copies of the issue cut out her article and passed it around.

It made us all look good. We had stood up to the administration. In the cafeteria, the *Owl* table got very popular for a couple of days. One black senior, James Colson, came over at lunch to compliment us. We grabbed him. We practically wrestled him to the ground. We begged him to be on the paper. He could do anything he wanted. He could have his own column. But he just laughed. He obviously thought the school newspaper was the geekiest thing you could possibly be involved with.

# 41

A couple of days later, I saw Cindy and Tara and some other girls standing around her locker. Cindy looked so cute. Her long blonde hair was pulled back and she had this tight sweater and jeans and white Jack Purcells. I waved as I passed her, but she pretended she didn't see. That bugged me. Why couldn't she smile at me once in a while?

That night I ate dinner with Drea and my mom. Drea told my mom about the recalling of the papers, and of course my mom freaked and wanted to call the principal to find out the details. I assured her it was over, everything was fine, we had handled it. I told her about Lydia Kresch standing up to everyone. My mom was not happy to hear that name. She did not want me getting sucked into some kind of trouble.

After dinner I went to my room to study, but I couldn't focus on anything. I picked up my phone and dialed Cindy's number. I still remembered it by heart.

"Hello," said Cindy.

I hesitated. "Hey," I said.

"Oh. It's you."

"How are you doing?" I asked.

"Fine."

I took a long, deep breath. Then I said the words. "Do you want to go out next Friday?"

There was silence.

"Like to a movie or something," I said. "Or . . . do you want to go watch the ice-skaters at Lloyd Center Mall?" She had liked to do that. She used to ice-skate when she was younger.

"Why are you asking me?"

"I want to see you. I want us to be . . . I don't want you to hate me anymore."

"I don't hate you."

"You avoid me."

"Of course I avoid you," she said sharply.

My chest filled with emotion. I didn't talk.

I could hear her breathe into the phone. "What time?" she said.

"I can pick you up. I have a car now."

"I know. What time?"

"Eight?"

"Okay." She hung up.


The next day was like a dream. I didn't tell anyone about the date. But I couldn't keep the smile off my face.

I sat with Kirk at lunch. He was talking to Peter and Bob Hollins about Becky Cetera. Kirk and Becky were together now. Or something. They had gone to Agenda together a couple of weekends in a row. Then one night they got drunk and made out in her parents' car. But now Becky Cetera was being very cool and noncommittal about the whole thing. She was very punk, very tough. Naturally, Kirk was hopelessly in love. "I knew this was going to happen," he said gloomily.

"Dude, you love it," said Peter.

"Dude, tell her to lose some weight," said Bob, biting into his sandwich.

Jill St. John came to our table. She was still working on her big tree-spiking article. It was so long we were going to chop it in half and run it in two issues. We needed pictures, though. Josh was willing to go on one of their midnight raids, but at the last minute his parents found out and wouldn't let him. So Jill was trying to get some pictures that her Anarcadia friends had taken.

But even problems were fun that day. Everything had an edge to it. *On Friday I was going out with Cindy.* It was like when we first started going out. I got this warm breathless feeling just thinking about it. And she had gotten even hotter than she was before. What would it be like to kiss her again? It would be incredible.

I forced myself not to think too far ahead. The immediate goal was to get things back to normal with her. Make it so we could say hi when we saw each other in the hall. She hadn't just been my girlfriend, she had been one of my best friends too. I wanted it back like that. Like it was. I would do it gradually. So no one would get hurt. And then whatever happened, happened.

This was what I told myself.

On Thursday I told Kirk. He couldn't believe it. He was stunned. "Jesus, you're going to break her heart all over again."

"We're just going to hang out. I'm going to go slow. It can't be any worse than it is now."

"Yes it can. You can hurt her. She's happy now. She's over you."

"If she's over me how come she can't talk to me? How come she can't look at me? How come she doesn't have another boyfriend?"

Drea thought it was a bad idea too.

"You're cruel," she said, from the floor of the TV room.

"Why do you say that?"

"She's not as strong as you. She's not the editor of the paper and surrounded by a million people. She only has herself. And Tara."

"She could have said no."

"Could she have?"

I called Lydia late that night. I was calling her a lot recently.

"I'm going out with Cindy tomorrow."

"What are you guys doing?"

"Going to Lloyd Center. Cindy likes to watch the ice-skaters."

"What are you going to say to her?"

"I don't know."

"That's very brave of you."

"I guess."

"Do you still love her?"

"I think I do. I don't think I ever stopped. All I know is, I'm really happy right now."

# 42

All week, before the date, I cleaned the third car. It smelled though. It had always smelled. I didn't know of what, mold, mildew, something. I normally kept one of those pine-scent Christmas-tree things hanging from my mirror. That week I put three more of them in various places around the car. I had to remember to take them out though. I would do it just before I left, for maximum effect.

On the night of the date, I went to my room to dress. I had set aside my favorite khakis, my favorite belt, my favorite shirt and sweatshirt and Nikes. Not that it mattered. Cindy knew what I looked like. It was mostly so I would feel my best. I got some extra money from my desk. I found some Certs, some gum.

At seven-forty, I went back to the car and took the pine-scent things out. I sniffed under the seats, in the back seat. It still smelled. Drea came out to put some clothes in the dryer. She watched me. She knew where I was going. She didn't say anything.

I drove to Cindy's. I parked in the street and walked to the door. This was going to be weird. Seeing her parents, her little brother Ben, their dog Rodney.

I rang the bell. I waited. I smoothed my hair. The door opened. It was Cindy. She didn't look at me. She yelled "Bye!" and slammed the door shut. We walked to my car in silence.

I opened the door for her. I walked around to my own side and got in.

"So this is my car," I said.

"I know. I've seen it in the parking lot."

I started the engine. "Yeah," I said. "It kinda sucks."

"It's all right."

"It smells," I said.

Cindy sniffed. "It smells like pine trees."


I suddenly felt worried about going to Lloyd Center Mall. I didn't know if that was enough of a date. What if we didn't have enough to talk about?

We pulled into the parking lot. I parked as close to the entrance as I could. When we walked in, I walked too fast. I made myself slow down.

We went to Cinnabon. Cindy ordered a cinnamon roll and a hot chocolate. I just got a hot chocolate. I didn't think I could eat a whole cinnamon roll, I was too nervous. Cindy couldn't eat it either. We sat at a booth in Cinnabon and took turns picking at it. We drank our hot chocolates.

"I never come here," said Cindy, meaning Lloyd Center.

"Yeah, it's kind of fun to come over here," I said. "I get sick of Woodridge Mall."

We went down to the lower level to watch the ice-skaters. There weren't many people skating. And most of them couldn't really skate. The reason I had suggested it was, when we first started going out, we went there one night and talked for hours. Now we weren't really talking. It was still okay though. It was nice to sit with her.

"You look nice," I said.

"Thanks."

"You look different lately."

"Do I?"

"You're dressing different," I said.

We sat there.

"Do you have a girlfriend?" she asked suddenly.

"No, of course not. You would know."

"Not if she went to another school."

"No, I don't."

Cindy looked forward.

"Do you?" I said.

"No."

I nodded. I watched the skaters. "But you went out with Charlton Hughes. That's what I heard."

She nodded that she had.

"How long did that last?"

"Not that long."

I laughed nervously. "What happened? Couldn't he get you into his sauna?"

"No," she said, frowning.

I looked away. I watched a little girl fall on the ice.

"I heard about you and Lydia Kresch," she said.

"Oh yeah. That was embarrassing."

"Did you guys go out?"

"No. God no. We played spin-the-bottle once. And then, check this out, her mom called my mom! Can you believe that?"

"She always sits at your table at lunch."

"Of course. She's our star columnist."

"I like her columns. They're funny."

"No, she's great. As a friend though, totally as a friend."

Watching the skaters got boring. So we walked around. We looked in the windows of the closed shops. There were other couples there. People on dates. They were sitting on benches, their legs over each other, their arms around each other. It was kind of awkward to see them.

So then Cindy suggested we go to her house to play Ping-Pong. It was an odd thing to suggest but somehow it seemed right. We went back to her house. Again, she kept her parents away. We went straight to their basement. She got us Diet Cokes and we played Ping-Pong. Then her brother Ben heard us and came down, and he and I played while Cindy watched. It was fun to see Ben. He couldn't care less that Cindy and I were hanging out again. He just wanted to play with someone who was half decent at Ping-Pong.

When Ben left, I sat with Cindy on the couch. I sat close. I let my shoulder touch her shoulder.

"You'd better go soon," she said, looking at her watch.

"Yeah," I said.

We sat there. Cindy studied her Diet Coke. "Can I ask you a question?" she said.

"Sure."

"Why did you ask me out tonight?"

I thought about my answer. "I'm not sure. I just wanted to see you."

"Do you want to get back together?"

"I was trying not to think that far ahead."

She nodded. "That's probably smart."

"Yeah," I said.

"But like when you leave? Are you going to try to kiss me? Like a normal date?"

"I wouldn't mind kissing you," I said.

Cindy stared at her Coke.

"Or not," I said. "If you don't want to."

"What would it mean though?"

"I don't know."

She thought about it. "If you're going to kiss me you should do it down here. Not upstairs."

"Like right now?"

She nodded.

I sat up. She wouldn't look at me but she turned and let me kiss her. Once. On the lips. Softly. Her mouth tasted wonderful, milky and warm.

After a few minutes we stopped. I put my arm around her. We didn't talk for a long time. My chest, my head, my whole body swelled with emotion.

It was like an ocean had been released inside me.

## 43

*Now I had everything.* That's how it felt. The paper, a car, *Cindy*.

I spent the next morning in my room working on my latest editorial. They had been terrible up until then, the usual crap about support your school and don't ruin the environment or whatever controversies were going on. Now I felt a new humor, a new lightness. I felt like I could do anything. I was complete in a way. I was at full strength.

That night, I went with Kirk to Agenda. I didn't call Cindy. I felt like I shouldn't rush it, I shouldn't force things.

We met Becky Cetera out front. She was a big Agenda person it turned out. She knew everyone. Brian Brain showed up later with Danielle and some of those people. I was polite to everyone but I was lost in my own thoughts. *I had Cindy back.*

As the night wore on I thought about other things. Like losing my virginity. I had never been obsessed with losing my virginity. I know everyone thinks you are, or you're supposed to be, when you're seventeen. But I was not. To me it was like puberty. Everyone reaches puberty. There are no adults who have not reached puberty. It was the same with sex. Everyone had sex. One night in front of the TV proved that. Getting your first time over with as soon as possible was one way to approach it. The other way was to take your time, make a good choice, and do it right. Cindy and I being each other's first would be doing it right. I had held out, I had not compromised, and now I was going to get my reward.

If I didn't screw it up.

On Sunday night I called Lydia. I told her about my date with Cindy.

"Wow," she said. "Your dream came true. You need to be careful though."

"What do you mean?"

"You need to know what you want from her."

"I want to go out with her again," I said.

"But why?"

"Because she's . . . she's Cindy, she's the girl I love."

"Why did you break up with her before?"

"I don't know." I thought about it. "I was just restless I guess."

Lydia didn't say anything.

"Actually, I wrote it down," I said, remembering an old notebook. "Let me see if I can find it."

I cradled the phone on my shoulder, and opened my desk drawer. I found the old notebook. I got it out. I read it to her:

*Reasons I broke up with Cindy.*

*1. We weren't talking.*

*2. It was getting painful to see her.*

*3. I felt tired when I was around her, relaxed and energetic when I wasn't.*

4. *I was going to be the editor of the paper next year and I needed more time.*

5. *I wanted to go to a good college, she didn't.*

6. *She ignored me at Gabby's party and shook up beer cans, and it seemed like she wanted to be friends with Gabby and Dominique.*

7. *She wanted to be a cheerleader which was a typical spur-of-the-moment decision which didn't make any sense. I was sick of trying to pretend like she was actually going to do things like that when I knew she wouldn't.*

After I finished Lydia didn't speak.

"What?" I said.

"Nothing."

"Do you think those are bad reasons to break up with someone?"

"No," said Lydia. "They're okay reasons."

"So why aren't you saying anything?"

"I'm thinking."

"What about?"

"Everything."

"Do you think I'm making a mistake?"

"I'm not sure."

At school, Kirk knew about my date with Cindy. No one else knew. At lunch, Cindy was sitting with Tara like she always did. During our year together we had had different lunchtimes. So it was strange to be in the cafeteria with her now. I didn't know where to sit.

I sat with Cindy. The people at the *Owl* table were like, *what?* Tara was also a little shocked to have me there. But she got over it. I think she was glad to see me, actually. Kirk came and sat with us too, which was nice. At the end of the lunch period, I had to go ask Jill St. John about her tree spiking pictures. It all felt pretty natural and okay: eat lunch with Cindy but still take care of *Owl* stuff.

# 44 - - - - - - - - - - - -

On Tuesday, I was in the *Owl* office most of the day. Jill St. John's story was so long, we were still editing it until the last minute. Lydia's latest column was also long, so we were moving stuff around. We now began "The New Rules" on the front page, with a little picture of Lydia above it.

I stayed late that night. When I got home I called Cindy, to check in, so she would know I would be a good boyfriend and call a lot. We talked for a bit. She had to help her mother with something, and I still had some calls to return, to Lydia, Kirk, Maria Sanchez. So we hung up.

On Wednesday I sat with Cindy at the cafeteria. It was weird sitting with her though, and not being at the *Owl* table. Later, Kirk and I were talking about the weekend and what kind of date Cindy and I should go on. Kirk suggested I bring Cindy to Agenda. He and Becky would come too. The four of us could go together.

So we tried that, Friday night. It was a little awkward. Cindy wasn't into downtown. She wasn't interested in the weird kids. We danced, and she seemed to like that. I bought her a smoothie and sat with her, and we watched people.

Then we went to Denny's, where you could get a huge plate of fries and gravy for three bucks. We talked and checked out the people coming through. Kirk and I eventually talked about newspaper stuff. And then Becky was laughing about the stupid "Voices" section which we were actually doing. Kirk was doing it. The first question was: "Do you matter?" The student respondents were baffled but Kirk thought it was hilarious. So did Becky. So we laughed about that. Cindy didn't say much. I tried to change the subject to non-*Owl* stuff but it didn't really work.

That night though, outside my house, Cindy and I made out in the Ford Explorer for like an hour. It got so intense we had to fold the back seat down. We didn't actually have sex, but it got very involved. Afterward we lay together, not talking. I touched her hair and neck. I wanted to tell her how much I loved her, but I kept thinking about what Lydia had said: to be careful. And what other people said: don't hurt her.

At school on Monday, people had suddenly heard about Cindy and me. Dominique Taylor came up to me in the hall.

"I heard," she announced. "You and Cindy. Back together!"

I smiled bashfully.

"I always said you were the perfect couple."

"I don't know about that."

"Maybe you don't, but I do," she said, striding away triumphantly.

# 45 - - - - - - - - - - - - - -

"Do you matter?" That was Kirk's "Voices" question. We had five people's responses and five pictures. I read through them:

> DARCY GRAVER (soph): "I matter to my friends."
>
> JOHN RODRIGUEZ (junior): "Not in a big way but in small ways I think I can help underprivileged people."
>
> NICHOLAS CHIN (senior): "I'm taking all AP science and hopefully if I continue to study I can contribute something in the sciences."
>
> MARY D'ANGELO (soph): "No. I mean, if I was never born everything would be the same pretty much, wouldn't it?"
>
> HOPE TRUMAN (frosh): "I matter to my mother. She's sick and she needs a special machine to keep her alive."

I went back to Mary D'Angelo. I'd never seen her before. I thought maybe she was one of Kirk's punk types, making a statement. But she wasn't. She was just some girl.

I told Kirk to cut Mary D'Angelo. He had a fit. He loved that she didn't think she mattered. "She's the only honest person in this whole school," he said. Kirk didn't think anyone mattered. Becky agreed. They were officially going out now. They were together all the time and having sex. She had spent a weekend at his house when his mom was visiting her sister in San Diego. I don't know where her parents were. Nowhere probably.

I talked to Lydia later about how people who dressed really punk or goth always had the worst home lives, or the most screwed-up parents. She agreed. She said she'd write a column about it.


I saw Drea that day after school. She usually got a ride or took the bus home, like I used to do. I grabbed her though and drove her home.

"To what do I owe this sudden burst of kindness?"

"Mary D'Angelo."

"Who's that?"

"Some girl."

I drove. Drea had heard about me and Cindy. She wanted to know more. "What's going to happen?" she asked.

"I'm not sure."

"But she's your girlfriend again?"

"I guess she is."

"You say that in a weird way."

"It's happening in a weird way."

- - -

I had a date with Cindy on Wednesday to go to a movie, but that was the day we ran the second installment of Jill's big tree-spiking piece, where they actually do the spiking. Naturally, Mr. Brown called a bunch of us into his office. We had all our arguments ready to defend ourselves, but it turned out Mr. Brown just wanted to make sure we were being careful. And we were.

Back at the *Owl* office everyone was kind of amped up by the meeting so we started debating other issues for the paper, like "Voices" and should we ask questions like "Do you matter?" It was an interesting question. Most people were against cutting out Mary D'Angelo's comment. What was the point of something like "Voices" if you didn't run the real comments? It was like *Cops*. The grim reality was the point.

Anyway, after all that I didn't get a chance to call Cindy until five-thirty, and by then she was about to eat dinner with her family. She sounded a little pissed. So I ended up going to McDonald's with Maria Sanchez and scientific Kevin.

That weekend was Thanksgiving. Cindy's family was going to Seattle to have dinner with her uncle. She called before she left, and we had a good talk about how things were going with us. We both agreed it was hard. She still felt unsure in some ways. It was hard for her to trust me. On my side, I felt like I had to overcompensate and be the perfect boyfriend, since I had hurt her the first time.

At one point I mentioned something about sex, but she

seemed reluctant to talk about it. Which was okay.

For the last twenty minutes the conversation drifted into more normal stuff. School stuff. Social stuff. It was more natural. That's what we were missing, just chatting casually. Like we used to. So that was good.

# 46

With Cindy in Seattle, I went to Agenda with Becky and Kirk. When we got inside I saw Ashley from Portland Episcopal. That was a surprise. I thought she might be doing an article. A lot of the high schools were doing articles about Agenda. It was "the new spot for hip teens" according to a recent *Sunday Oregonian*. Ashley said she went there a lot. She was kind of snobby about it. Like this was *her* place. She was hard to deal with.

Also Danielle was there. She told me Eleanor had moved to L.A. to live with her mom for a while. I passed this news on to Kirk. He didn't say anything. But he missed her. We all did. Danielle most of all. She didn't seem to have anyone to talk to. She kept coming back to our table. And sitting next to me.

Cindy got back from Seattle, and on Tuesday we went to the first basketball home game of the season. Everyone was there; it was a tradition. When Cindy and I walked in together, people yelled and clapped. They high-fived us as we climbed up the bleachers to the student section. Apparently all was right with the world when Cindy and I were a couple.

Tara showed up, and she sat with us. Dominique Taylor and Gabby Greenberg and some other people were behind us. Then I saw Nathan. He was sitting behind Dominique. I wondered where Lydia was. I realized Lydia had not said anything about Nathan in several weeks. I had assumed there was still something going on between them.

Then Roberta Handel walked in, with Sonya Taylor and the rest of their cute freshmen posse. People went crazy. Everyone was hooting and yelling and throwing stuff. Roberta loved it, you could tell.

They saw Nathan and Dominique and started coming up the bleachers. People made room and they took their seats. Roberta sat right beside Nathan. She was doing her shy, bashful act. I swear, I don't think I ever saw her speak. She just smiled her plastic smile and allowed people to adore her.

The game started. No one really paid attention. Bryce was with his new girlfriend from Portland Episcopal. He had a new sophomore guy who wrote all the sports articles now. That's what happened when you were a senior and you finally had some power. You had other people do your work for you.

## 47

Nathan and Roberta. Somehow, that week, they became an official couple. It made perfect sense. They were each the most popular people in their class.

Lydia, though, was suddenly nowhere to be found. She came into the *Owl* office only once all week and didn't seem to be anywhere else either. I called her at home on Thursday. I wasn't sure how to bring it up. "So what happened with Nathan?" I said.

"We broke up."

"Huh," I said.

"To be honest, I'm not sure we were ever going out," she said. Her voice was quiet.

"I'm sorry."

"At least he called. He was very nice. He said he liked Roberta. He didn't think it was a big deal. I guess it wasn't."

"That sucks."

"It was fun having the most popular guy in school for a boyfriend. Or almost having him. That's pretty superficial though, isn't it?"

"Yeah, but whatever."

"How's Cindy?"

"Good."

"You guys are good together."

"I guess. It's been kind of hard."

"At least you have someone," said Lydia.

"Yeah, but you'll find someone else."

"Will I?"

"Of course," I assured her. "There's a million guys you could go out with. You gotta come to class though."

"I know," she said.

"Come to the *Owl* office tomorrow. You can hide there."

"I will. I was too embarrassed. I wrote a column about him."

"Everyone gets dumped. It will make people like you more. Lydia Kresch, star columnist, has problems too."

"*Star columnist*," she said.

"You're going to rule the world someday. What do you care about Nathan Reimer? This is nothing."

"Do you think I'm going to rule the world?"

"You already rule Evergreen."

"No, I don't. But thanks for saying it."

That evening after dinner, my mom and I were in the kitchen. She asked if I knew who Billy Hutchinson was.

I didn't.

"Drea has a date with him," said my mom. "I don't know if I should let her go."

I snuck a look at Drea, who was clearing the table. "Really?" I said.

The next morning in the car, Drea was annoyed.

"So," I said, as I pulled the car out of the driveway.

"I know, Mom told you about Billy. God, I can't believe

she's making a big deal out of this. You went out with girls freshman year."

"No, I didn't."

"She wasn't going to let me go. Even though Marcy's mother is going to drive us. It's four people. To a movie. It's so stupid. Who cares?"

At school, I made Kevin take me to the frosh/soph wing between classes and show me Billy Hutchinson's locker.

"So what's the deal with this guy?" I asked him.

"I dunno."

"Who is he?"

"He's just some guy."

"What's he *like*?"

"He's a freshman. He has glasses."

"Does he have girlfriends?"

"I seriously doubt it."

"Find out for me."

I told Cindy about it and her eyes lit up. She liked Drea. She had never heard of Billy Hutchinson. She wanted to find out who he was. We both wandered through the cafeteria during underclassmen lunch but there were a million freshmen with glasses.

I told Lydia, and she didn't know who my sister was. I walked with her into the frosh/soph wing and pointed out Drea.

"*That's* your sister?"

"Yeah, what's wrong with her?"

"Nothing. I didn't know you had a sister. You never told me."

"Well I do and that's her."

"I'll look out for her."

"Find out who Billy Hutchinson is."

So I had my spies out. I wasn't doing it for my mom. I had no intention of passing on anything I found out. It was more for Drea. If she really liked this guy maybe I could help. And the more I knew, the better off I'd be. Knowledge is power.

# 48 - - - - - - - - - - - - - - -

Nathan won the cross-country championship that weekend. Everybody was pretty psyched, though it wasn't like before when no one knew who he was. Now he was in the *Oregonian* all the time. He was on TV. It was more fun rooting for him when he was our own little secret.

That same weekend Cindy and I were supposed to do something. At the last minute she called and said she had to hang out with Tara. So then Bob Hollins invited me over to play poker.

The poker game was a classic "night with the guys" situation. We listened to AC/DC and Guns and Roses and a lot of bad classic rock. We drank beer. Bob had some cigars, though nobody could really stand to smoke them.

I called Cindy later, as the game was winding down. She was leaving Tara's and said we could meet up. That sort of saved the night. Especially since I had lost twenty bucks at poker.

I met Cindy in the Safeway parking lot by her house. She could only stay for a few minutes. We totally made out in the back of her Ford Explorer. There was something desperate and crazy about it. We barely spoke. We just grabbed each other like never before.

Afterward we had to untangle ourselves and find our shoes and other articles of clothing. At the next opportunity we would totally have sex. It was obvious.

She had to rush home because she was so late. I watched the Ford Explorer go bouncing out of the Safeway parking lot.

That Saturday, Drea went out with Billy Hutchinson. They went to a movie with her friend Marcy and another boy. They saw a matinee movie at Woodridge Mall. Then they went for ice cream. This was all according to my mom.

On Monday, I had Drea to myself, in the car.

"So?" I said.

"So what?"

"How was Billy?"

"None of your business. Oh and thanks for making Kevin come snooping around about him. That was really stupid."

"I didn't make Kevin do anything. I just asked him. He's a sophomore, I thought he would know."

"And Lydia Kresch has been smiling at me. As if."

"As if what?"

"As if she's going to be friends with me."

"Why not?"

"Because she's so famous now. And friends with you."

We stopped at a red light across the street from school. Several students were standing at the corner, waiting to cross. A tall freshman boy glanced over at us. He saw Drea. A big smile broke across his face.

He was Billy Hutchinson.

He waved and started to approach our car. Drea waved him away and then tried to pretend she hadn't.

"Is that him?"

"Can you please not say anything?"

"Can I meet him?"

"No. *Please.*"

"All right, all right."

I pulled across the street. I dropped Drea off and parked. I stayed in my car though and watched him come through the parking lot. He seemed okay: a tall, skinny freshman. He had glasses, curly longish hair, the face of a child.

It was the beginning of December now. I had begun to think about Christmas presents for Cindy. I was thinking of buying her a ring. I told Kirk, but he thought a ring was too serious.

"Maybe that's what I want," I said.

"Dude, you're not getting engaged to Cindy Sherman. You're not going to marry her, you're not going to do *anything* with her. You're going to graduate and go to some fancy college and get some fancy job and everything you did here will be forgotten. End of story."

"That's not true."

"Don't kid yourself. End of story."

## 49

Becky Cetera was one of those people at school who sneak up on you. She was short and kind of heavy, she wore punk shoes and dresses, and her hair was dyed yellow. Of course by now probably twenty percent of all high school students were punk or "emo" or had their hair dyed or something. So that wasn't particularly unusual.

When she started coming to the *Owl*, I barely noticed her. She had signed up and was getting credit; she wasn't the type to give away her time for free. There was something tenacious about her though, so initially we had her proofread and do other important stuff. She was good at everything you asked her to do. But she was tough. She wouldn't do proofreading after the first month. She told us to get someone else to do it.

It was at Agenda that Becky really shone. She was a big Agenda girl. She was a downtown girl generally, but not like

Eleanor, she was a different type, a harder type. Becky's Agenda girlfriends worked at Metro Mall or the shops downtown. For them it was all about makeup and clothes and being mean to boys, especially if you liked them.

This was what I was thinking one night while she and I waited for Kirk to get beer. Becky was in the front passenger seat. I was in the back seat. We were on our way to a party. We had stopped at the store where the guy would sell you beer if you gave him five bucks. I hadn't been on one of these beer runs in a while. Cindy didn't like beer. Becky drank a forty every weeknight, and more on weekends.

Kirk came back. He handed me two six-packs and I jammed them under Becky's seat. Since I became editor I didn't like to do stuff that was blatantly illegal. It didn't look good. But somehow Becky's presence made it seem important. Like I would be too much of a wuss if I couldn't handle a beer run.

We drove. It was a Hillside party we were going to. I had invited Cindy to go but she passed. We were having that problem again. She didn't like to do stuff I liked, in this case go to a Hillside party, which tended to be pretty skanky. Hillside parties usually got busted or someone got in a fight or some guy who graduated three years ago would try to sell you drugs.

As Kirk said, they had a certain "car crash" quality to them. Which was exactly what made them fun.

It wasn't that great though. Julie, Kirk's friend, was there. She was really drunk as usual. Becky found some girls she knew. Kirk and I ended up in the basement playing foosball.

When we got upstairs again, Becky introduced me to a girl she knew. She pushed us together and said, "You two should go out." The girl seemed nice, but I was with Cindy. What was I supposed to do? I made an excuse and walked away. I found Becky and Kirk across the room.

"In case you forgot, I have a girlfriend," I told Becky.

"Yeah?" said Becky. "So where is she?"

Before we left, I found a phone and called Cindy on her cell phone.

"Can we meet up tonight?" I whispered.

"Uhm . . . "

"What?"

"I don't think so," she said.

"Why not?"

"I don't like meeting in parking lots."

"Well, I don't either," I said. "But I thought . . . "

"What did you think?"

"I thought that's what you wanted."

"Is that what you want?" she asked.

"Of course not. . . . I want you to come out with me. But if you won't do anything. . . . If you have to hang out with Tara every second. . . ."

"I don't *have* to hang out with Tara."

"Well, what's happening then?"

"You tell me."

# 50 - - - - - - - - - - - - -

Cindy changed her mind. We decided to meet. In the Safeway parking lot.

I drove there fast. I talked to myself, practicing what I would say: *Why won't you do things with me? Why don't you support me more? Why can't you take some interest in the* Owl *and my friends . . . ?*

I drove fast. I was pissed. I felt like Cindy owed me. Ever since we got back together, I had been the perfect boyfriend. When she didn't want to hang out I never complained, even when she flaked at the last second. This whole time I had been extra careful, extra nice, extra everything.

I saw the Ford Explorer. It was off to one side of the parking lot. I drove to it and stopped. I got out. I slammed my door shut.

Cindy was standing beside the Explorer, her arms crossed. As I approached her, she touched her face. She was crying.

I wasn't expecting that. "Why are you crying?" I said.

"Why do you think?"

I stood over her. There was something wrong in her face. This was supposed to be an argument about our future, our relationship, the ways we were going to change our relationship.

"I don't know," I said. I was still pissed.

"I can't do this anymore."

The words ripped through my chest like bullets. "What?"

She blinked her eyes. She covered her mouth.

"What part can't you do any more?" I said.

"Any of it."

"Wait . . . you want to . . . break up?"

She nodded. Then she shook her head violently.

"But I love you," I said. "And I thought—"

"It isn't working. You know it isn't. It's like you said the other time. I love you too, but it doesn't work."

"What doesn't work? What?"

She shook her head. She cried more. I stepped closer.

"We just need time," I said. "And we have to talk more."

She shook her head.

"And we can't break up," I said, trying to smile. "We're going to be each other's first . . ."

She looked at the ground and shook her head harder. "We can't do that either," she said. "I already had sex with Charlton."

I stared at her. "But that's not possible. I thought you said—"

"I didn't say anything."

"You did, you—"

"You just assumed it," she said. "Because that's what *you* wanted."

"But . . . " I said. I stepped back. "But Charlton? He's such a—"

"I'm not *proud* of it!" she said, with sudden anger. "God! I hate him now. I hated him then."

"But why did you—?"

"Because you dumped me!" she hissed. "Because you walked away from me after I gave you everything! And I would have given you that too if you'd let me. How was I supposed to know what to do? You're the great Max Caldwell. You're the one who knows everything. . . ." She dissolved into tears.

I stepped backward. I walked backward to my car. Then I turned and got in it and drove away.

# Part Four Winter

Christmas was kind of a blank that year. My family and I went to church on Christmas Eve and then came home and watched TV—Drea and I did anyway. I didn't really sleep that night, and then woke up early and waited for other people to get up. My dad went downstairs first and started a fire. Then I heard Drea go downstairs, and my mom. I got up and put on my bathrobe.

My mom had doughnuts out. And some Christmas music on the stereo. Drea and I sat around the tree and opened presents, which were all pretty low-key, since we were older now. I gave my dad a sweater. Mom gave Drea a video about soccer. My dad gave me a new computer program that had every school-related thing you could ever need on it. Dictionary, thesaurus, synopses of classic books, outlines for term papers. It was for college. I sure wasn't going to need it next semester. High school, as far as I was concerned, was over.

It rained the whole day, of course, and then froze that

night, which fouled up traffic. Highway 26 was a huge traffic jam. It was all over the news.

The next day Kirk and Becky came by and rescued me. We went to the movies at Woodridge Mall. It was weird hanging out with them though. Kirk tended to talk less when he was with Becky. There were a lot of long silences.

On New Year's Eve I was supposed to meet Kirk and Becky at Agenda, but there was more black ice on the roads, and my parents wouldn't let me take the car. That sucked. But I didn't really feel like going out anyway. I walked to the 7-Eleven and watched people yell and honk their horns in the parking lot.

On the Sunday after New Year's, Ashley Cole had an open house party. Peter Daley wanted someone to go with, so I went. Corinne was there, the girl we played tennis with. We were talking to her and then Ashley came over. She had just been accepted early decision to Barnard College in New York City. She was very excited about it. She said she couldn't picture herself anywhere else, no other location compared to Manhattan.

"Yeah, it's kind of the biggest city," I said.

"How about you, what are you doing with colleges?"

"Just applying. You know."

Peter and Corinne wandered away.

"You should have applied early decision," said Ashley. "That shows them you know what you want."

"Yeah."

"I've been meaning to ask you something, by the way," she said, squinting at me strangely. "How come you've never asked me out? I mean like on a real date."

I shrugged. "I didn't know you wanted me to."

"*I* invited *you* over for dinner."

"I guess I thought we'd see each other around."

"I hate how guys do that. They sniff around but they can't follow through on things. It's quite annoying."

"I had a girlfriend actually. I mean, I still liked my old girlfriend."

"Oh yeah? And what happened with that?"

"We tried to get back together but . . . it didn't work out."

"Oh you *retro-dated*. That never works. Everyone knows that."

"Yeah, I guess."

"Well, it's too late now because I'm seeing someone."

I nodded.

"But maybe next year," she said, waving to someone behind me. "If you're back east. And, you know, if I'm not too busy."


On the last Saturday of vacation, Kirk and I went downtown and hung out at the Air Hockey Café. Becky came down and joined us, and some of her friends were there. One girl, Monica, kept talking to me even though I didn't really say much back. I guess she just liked to talk. She was kind of weird anyway. Someone called her on her cell phone and she went outside where she could hear better. I watched her through the window. I watched Becky and Kirk play air hockey. Then I went home.

# 52 - - - - - - - - - - - -

Two weeks later, on a rainy January night, I was sitting on the couch in Becky Cetera's living room. Her parents were gone, and some Agenda people had come over. Kirk, Becky, and another girl were on the floor looking through a box of vinyl records they had found at a garage sale. They were playing some of them on an old record player Brian Brain had brought over. I was sitting on the couch behind them, drinking a beer.

Danielle came and sat down next to me. "Hey," she said. "You're awfully quiet tonight."

I shrugged.

"Did you go to Agenda last weekend?"

"No," I said. It was weird about Danielle. We had the same conversation every time we talked. What's up? Been to Agenda lately? Any news from Eleanor? I had realized that Danielle wasn't even that close of friends with Eleanor. Danielle wasn't really close friends with anyone. She was just this strange girl who attached herself to things.

"Agenda is getting so suburban," she said. "I wish some new place would open."

I drank my beer. Danielle had a denim skirt on, and a tight T-shirt with no bra. You could totally see her breasts. She obviously wanted you to.

Kirk walked by on his way to the kitchen. "Hey Max, c'mere a sec," he said.

I got up and followed him into the kitchen.

"What's going on with Danielle?" he said in a low voice.

"Nothing," I said. "We're talking."

He nodded. "You know she'd go upstairs with you. If you want."

"How do you know?"

"She's talking to you isn't she?"

"Yeah, so?"

"She's into you, she's always been into you."

"Are you sure?"

"Yeah. Totally."

I looked back at Danielle. She was still sitting on the couch, waiting for me to come back.

"I'm just saying, if you want to," continued Kirk, quietly.

"No," I said. "Maybe you're right."

"You gotta move on it though. She won't wait around forever."

I nodded. Kirk had taken a bottle of Jack Daniel's out of the freezer. He poured a shot's worth into the bottom of a glass. "Here," he said. "Drink that."

I picked up the glass. I smelled it. It was very strong.

"And take this." He stuffed something into my front jeans pocket. "Don't take it out. It's a condom."

I nodded. "So what do I do?"

"Ask her if she wants to go upstairs. Then take her to Becky's room."

"But what's my excuse?"

"You don't need an excuse."

"But like, go upstairs to do what?"

"Just go upstairs. Just say, *Do you want to go upstairs?*"

"Okay."

"Repeat it back."

"Do you want to go upstairs," I said.

"That's it. Nothing else. And don't start talking about the weather."

I lifted the Jack Daniel's to my mouth. I drank it. It was awful.

I went back to Danielle. I had two glasses of whiskey and Coke. I gave one to her. "I wanted to get you a drink," I said.

"Oh, thank you," she said. She took a sip of it. "So where were we?"

"Agenda," I said. But then I cleared my throat. "Actually, do you wanna . . . do you want to go upstairs?"

She looked at me. "Right now?" she said.

I nodded.

"And do what?" she asked.

"Just whatever."

She watched me for a moment. Then a mischievous smile came over her face. "All right," she said.

Going up the stairs, I was so nervous I thought I was going to throw up. I walked behind Danielle. Her wide, flat hips were in front of me. And her thin legs. She was wearing black nylons and these strange red tennis shoes that had one stripe. The stairway itself was narrow. It was carpeted, with fake wood paneling on the sides. I slipped at one point on the carpeting. I almost spilled my whiskey and Coke.

At the top of the stairs, Danielle looked back at me and smiled again. I tried to smile back.

We went down the hall. We found Becky's room. We went inside. I didn't know if I should leave the light on or not. I left it on.

Danielle sat on the bed. "God," she said. "It's about time. I thought you were never going to do anything."

"Sorry," I said. I sat next to her. She helped me take my coat off, and the sweater under it.

Then she scooted close to me. She kissed me on the mouth. Her tongue went immediately inside mine and darted around. I could barely keep up with it. Meanwhile, her hand touched my arm, then my chest, then my thigh.

We eased back on the bed and I crawled on top of her. I did everything you're supposed to do: I felt her chest, her legs, between her legs. She slipped a hand under my shirt and lightly caressed the small of my back. A gigantic shiver passed through my entire body.

# 53 - - - - - - - - - - - - - -

Danielle was pretty cool about everything, considering she had to do all the important stuff, like getting the condom on right side up. She didn't mention the fact that I was trembling the whole time. And she didn't complain when it lasted all of about forty-five seconds.

Afterward, she smoked a cigarette while I stared at the ceiling. Then she began stroking my hair. I think she wanted to fool around some more, but she could see I was too freaked out. So she lit another cigarette, smoked it, and then got out of bed.

She put on her clothes. I watched her from the bed. She was five years older than me. She didn't have any normal friends. She wasn't pretty. We had never had a meaningful conversation. Watching her, I felt like I was a different person. I wasn't Max Caldwell anymore. Max Caldwell would never be in that room.

Danielle finished dressing. "Are you going to stay here?" she said.

"Oh, no. . . ." I said. I got up and hurriedly put on my pants. I was still clutching the used condom in my fist. There was no place to put it, so I jammed it into the pocket of my coat.

I followed Danielle down the stairs to the living room. People were still mostly in the living room. Danielle joined the other girls who were sitting around the record player. I didn't know what to do. Go with her? Wait? I stepped into the kitchen. I watched Danielle from there. I wondered if she was going to leave. I hoped she would.

I got my wish. Danielle went into another room and came back with her coat, which was purple suede and had white fur around the collar. She said something to Becky, who kissed her good-bye.

Then she came toward me. "I'm going now," she said.

"Okay," I said. "I'll walk you to your car."

"You don't have to," she said as she buttoned her coat.

"No, I will."

"Really, you don't have to."

"Don't you want me to?" I asked.

She didn't answer. I followed her to the door anyway. She opened it and went out. I went out behind her. I thought, *I should kiss her good-bye on the front step*.

But she never turned around. She kept walking: down the steps, along the cement path, down the wet driveway to the street. I watched her from the door. She pulled her collar up as she walked. Her purse swung from her elbow. The Ceteras had one of those little lawn lanterns: it lit her back as she disappeared into the drizzly night.

I closed the door, but with me on the outside. In the quiet of the suburban neighborhood, I could hear Danielle's footsteps moving away down the street. I heard her car door open. I heard it shut. The engine started and she drove away.

I sat on the step, my forearms across my knees. The outside world now was perfectly still, perfectly quiet. The tiny drops of moisture in the air swirled in the lamplight.

> *Your arms full, and your hair wet, I could not*
> *Speak, and my eyes failed, I was neither*
> *Living nor dead, and I knew nothing,*
> *Looking into the heart of light, the silence.*

A few minutes later the door opened behind me. It was Kirk. He had a whiskey and Coke. He handed me the glass. "How did it go?" he said.

I didn't answer. I took the drink and took a big sip of it. It tasted horrible, but it helped me somehow. I drank some more. I drank the whole glass.

"Whoa dude, easy there," said Kirk.

A brutal, burning sensation worked its way through my chest. My eyes burned and my brain numbed completely for a moment. But then it passed. And then everything was all right. And Kirk was there. And I wasn't a virgin anymore.

# 54 - - - - - - - - - - - - -

But I still had to get home. I had to *drive* home. I could barely get the key in the ignition. I was *so drunk*.

I got the engine started. I turned on the heater. But I

didn't trust myself. I went around the dashboard and double-checked everything: lights on, engine on, parking brake off, windshield wipers on, seat belt buckled.

When everything seemed okay, I pulled away from the curb. I drove very slowly. It was hard to see in the drizzle and fog. I turned the windshield wipers up to full speed. I turned on the radio.

I avoided the highway, which would have been quickest. Instead I went the back way. It took half an hour. Even that was hard. The most simple things were difficult: steering straight, remembering to signal, slowing down for stop signs. But gradually I got more comfortable. The radio played, the car filled with warmth from the heater. I took deep breaths.

I got to my own neighborhood. It was two-thirty in the morning; an hour and a half past my curfew. *And my dad was home*, I suddenly remembered. He might even be waiting up.

I drove faster. I steered down my street. I would park out front and quietly sneak up into my room. But that would arouse suspicion. The third car traditionally stayed in the garage.

So I decided to try something Kirk often did. I would accelerate until I had enough speed. Then I'd cut the engine and coast silently up the driveway and into my spot.

The problem with that plan: the Honda had power brakes. Without the engine on, they barely worked. That's what I forgot. The other problem was that I was watching the front of the house as I swung into the driveway. I was trying to see if my parents' bedroom light was on. What if my dad was waiting up? That's what I was thinking about when I put my foot on the brake.

And that's the last thing I remember.


It was loud. It must have been very loud.

The garage lights were on when I regained consciousness. My father was trying to wake me up. I was trying to wake up too. My mother was there. And Drea. My door wouldn't open. My dad got in the back seat, and crawled into the front. He put his leg across my lap and kicked my door open. Looking down at his leg was when I saw the blood all over my front. I touched my mouth and a sharp pain flashed through my nose and face.

I had broken my nose.

They got me out of the car. It was hard to walk. The car was jammed in under my dad's wood shop table. Stuff was scattered everywhere, on the floor, across the hood of the Honda, which was totally mangled. You could see long white splinters of wood where the car had destroyed the underpart of the wood shop. You could see where the front bumper had smashed through the back of the garage.

They brought me inside and sat me on the couch. Preparations were made to drive me to the hospital. My mother was totally freaked, needless to say. She went through my coat pockets and promptly found the used condom. She pulled it out for all to see. That was a nice moment. Drea, in her pajamas, watched the whole thing from behind my parents. There was a sad, distant look in her face.

My dad inspected my bleeding face. My mom bent down and looked closely into my eyes. "Look at him!" she said. "He's on drugs! Look at his eyes!"

"He's drunk," said my dad calmly.

"He's heartbroken," said Drea, quietly. I don't think my parents even heard her. But I did. It made me close my eyes for a moment, close them and then open them again very slowly.

My dad took me to the hospital. My nose was broken. My lips were cut up. The old Honda didn't have an air bag. The good news was, I hadn't lost any teeth. "At your age, the teeth are the important thing," joked the doctor. "Unless you were planning to be a model."

I didn't laugh. The doctor was nice though. Everyone was nice. The doctor seemed to like my dad. They were both in the sciences. They understood each other.

When I got home, my mother was waiting. She was very upset. I had this big plastic brace taped over my nose, so it was easy to close my eyes and avoid facing her.

Drea had gone to bed. My dad helped me upstairs and took off my pants and shirt for me. They had given me painkillers, but once I lay down I was wide awake. I stared out my window at the tall evergreen trees across the street. I could feel the plastic of the steering wheel like it was still embedded in my face.

# 55

The brace protector thing they put on my nose made me look like Frankenstein. Frankenstein with a nose job gone terribly wrong. As for the rest of my face: My eyes swelled up and turned orange and blue and purple. My lips swelled up and scabbed over. My nose was twice its normal size. My head had a rotten grapefruit quality.

For the next couple of days, I took painkillers and slept and watched TV. My mom made me soup. I started to feel better. But I didn't go to school. My mom stayed home too.

On Tuesday I snuck to my computer and checked my e-mail. People at school had heard about the accident and wished me well: Kirk, Becky, Lydia, Peter Daley. Maria Sanchez was in charge of the *Owl* in my absence. And Bryce. Maria offered to send me some articles to read, when I was ready.

On Wednesday my mom went to work, and I had the house to myself. I took a bath and soaked in the hot water. I thought about Danielle. It was my first chance to be alone with myself and my thoughts about her. I opened my mind to it. I thought about everything: the party, Kirk, Danielle, being in Becky's room. But I didn't feel anything. There was nothing there. No sense of satisfaction or even regret. It seemed strange to feel so empty. I didn't trust it. It didn't seem like a good thing.

- - -

On Thursday I wanted to go back to school. But my parents wouldn't let me. The doctor had said to stay home a week.

A tow truck came around lunchtime and I watched them try to get the Honda out of the garage. It was embedded in the back wall. The tow truck guy saw my face and said, "This your work, chief?"

I spent the rest of the day on my computer, answering e-mails and instructing Maria Sanchez to cut the last paragraph off Lydia's column.

At dinner I pumped Drea for news about school, but got nothing interesting. My mom had remained curiously quiet all that week. That was not good. Kirk called that night. He said Becky had called Danielle but all she said was, "I told him not to drink so much."

Lydia called too. I told her she needed to cut the last paragraph off her new column but she just laughed. "You always want to cut the last paragraph off my columns." It was true. I did that a lot. I had read somewhere that that's what they did at *The New Yorker*. "You just worry about getting better," said Lydia. "I'll worry about my last paragraphs."

On Friday I got an e-mail from Cindy:

> *Max—*
> *Heard about your accident. Hope you're okay.*
> *Everyone's hoping you are.*
> *Cindy*

I read it several times. Then I deleted it.

- - -

On Friday night, my father and mother came into the TV room. They sent Drea upstairs (though I knew she was probably listening somehow). They turned off the TV.

They told me that drinking and driving was a very serious crime. That I could have killed someone, killed myself, killed one of them. Did I understand that?

I said I did.

They were not going to ground me. They felt like such a punishment would trivialize what I had done. But they were not going to replace the third car, since it was totaled and since I had demonstrated such poor judgment in having it. So that was one form of punishment. Besides that, the damage I'd done to my future and to myself was probably punishment enough.

I nodded that I understood.

Then my mom looked at me. "If you need help, if you think you have a problem with drugs or alcohol, you need to tell us. There are people who can help you."

I said I didn't think I did. I didn't usually drink that much.

"People who have problems tell themselves they don't have problems," said my mother.

"The only problem I have is . . ." I started to say.

"What?" said my mother.

But I couldn't think of how to finish it.

"What's the only problem you have?" my father asked.

I shrugged. I didn't know. I shook my head.

- - -

So they sent me to Dr. Sorensen.

I went Saturday morning. My mother dropped me off at the clinic downtown. She stayed double-parked in front to make sure I went in. Like what was I going to do, run away? With my Frankenstein mask on?

It was my mom's way of saying, *I don't know you anymore.*

# 56

"Hello, Max."

"Hello, Dr. Sorensen."

I sat in the chair in front of his desk. Dr. Sorensen was looking at some papers. He put them aside and smiled at me.

"Looks like you've got yourself an injury there."

"I broke my nose," I said. I noticed for the first time that my voice had a ridiculous nasal tone. I sounded like a pig.

"How did that come about?"

"I lost my virginity," I said. "And then I got drunk and crashed my car."

He watched me. "That's an interesting series of events."

"I guess. My parents weren't too into it."

"I would hope not."

I sat there.

"Why don't we talk about it."

We did. We talked about what happened. We talked about the different people involved. It didn't really lead to anything though. Besides talking about my childhood, my ambivalence, my "coping mechanisms."

"What if I can't love anyone the right way?" I finally said.

"What do you mean, Max?"

"I loved Cindy from the day I met her. And look at what's happened. She's heartbroken, I'm heartbroken, I got this thing on my face."

"Perhaps it's the nature of love," said Dr. Sorensen, "to defy our understanding."

That was typical Dr. Sorensen. It sounded good but it didn't really answer the question.


That weekend was pretty tense. My parents were watching me very closely. They could see that I was not sorry. I was not horrified that I had driven the third car into the back of the garage. I was not acting like it was the worst thing that a seventeen-year-old kid ever did. I was not begging for forgiveness, or worrying it would jeopardize my college chances, or any of the things they thought I should do.

The reality was, I didn't care. I mean, I did. I tried to. I went out with my dad and helped prop his shop table back up. But even then, the feeling between us was cold and far away. Something had happened. I had somehow moved outside my parents' sphere of influence. It was not about them anymore. It was about me.

- - -

On Monday I missed another day of school to go to a drug and alcohol counselor. Dr. Sorensen had told my parents that my personality fit some youth-at-risk profile, mostly the racing brain thing and my tendency to obsess and "over-focus." Apparently people who worry a lot become drug addicts.

My dad was relatively cool about it though. He drove me to the clinic. He believed me when I said I didn't drink that much, but he said seeing the guy would reassure everyone.

But it wasn't that reassuring. For starters, the counselor I talked to was really smart. Like creepy smart. He seemed to know me. Like just talking in his office, I felt like he was reading my mind. Then he opened my file and looked at it for a while. He said, "When you get this *racing brain* Dr. Sorensen talks about, where exactly does your brain race *to*?"

"I don't know," I said. "All over the place."

"Positive places or negative places?"

"More negative I guess."

"For instance, if, say, you have some normal problem, your homework is late, something minor, does that thing tend to grow in your mind, when you're having the 'racing brain'? Maybe it gets bigger than it really should?"

"Yeah, I guess so."

"And how big does it get?"

"Pretty big."

"Like sometimes, so big you feel like . . . you would do anything to stop it?"

"No. Not that big," I said. "I mean . . . maybe . . . sometimes."

"Do you always bite your nails?" he said, closing the file.

I was biting them at that moment. I put my hand down.

Later I went into a cubicle and took a written test. It had questions like: Do you drink on school nights? Do you drink alone? Do you drink to feel better about yourself? I answered no to all of them.

All I really wanted was to get back to work on the *Owl*. Another whole issue was done and I still wasn't there.

Finally, on Tuesday, my mom drove Drea and me to school. Of course people were all over me, checking out my face, gawking at me, whatever. At lunch everyone wanted to see my stitches, so I took my Frankenstein mask off and showed them.

Cindy wasn't around. I swear she had ways to make herself invisible. It pissed me off, since in a way, it was all for her. . . .

# 57 - - - - - - - - - - - - -

By the end of the week, things were getting back to normal. I spent two days writing an editorial about the corrupt food company that supplied our cafeteria. It was boring though.

That weekend Kirk and I went downtown to the Air Hockey Café. Kirk finally got me to order a Depth Charge.

My face was a lot better now. I'd stopped wearing the plastic brace and was putting a Band-Aid over the stitches. It itched though. My whole face itched so bad sometimes I had to jam my hands in my pockets and hum to myself.

On Monday, my parents' insurance guy called. They were raising our whole family's car insurance eight hundred dollars a year.

And then later that week my mother came into the TV room while Drea and I were watching *ER*. Out of nowhere she started yelling at me for taking the nose brace off. I wasn't supposed to. She was so upset I finally went upstairs and found the brace and taped it back onto my face.

But it was obvious she was frustrated about other things. She didn't believe I was truly sorry for what had happened. I had gotten off easy. I didn't properly realize what I had done.

Also, there was the used condom. She'd never said a word about it.

Kirk and I went downtown on Friday night. Kirk drove. We met Becky and her friend Monica. She was only fifteen, it turned out, but she seemed a lot older than that. She was always talking on her cell phone. And then when she hung up she'd tell some outrageous story about the person she was just talking to.

First we went to Agenda, but it was closed. Then we drove around. Then we went to Monica's house and hung out in her basement. It was kind of weird there. Her sister was having a fight with her dad and you could hear them yelling upstairs.

We started watching *Hellraiser 3* on video, which was terrible, and then Kirk and Becky slunk off to some other room, probably to have sex. Which left Monica and me alone on the couch.

That's when I decided to try for Monica. She had been touching her knee to mine in the car and kind of looking at me a lot, even when she was on her phone. So I went for it. I started kissing her. At first she hesitated, but once we got going she was all over me. She tried to undo my belt. I wouldn't let her though. Fortunately Kirk and Becky came back.

On Monday my mom took me back to the doctor and he took the stitches out. They X-rayed me too, to make sure my nose bones were healing correctly. Afterward, driving home, my mom told me that if colleges found out about what happened I could lose my chance to go to an Ivy League college. Which was crap. My applications were in. Nothing I did now was going to change anything.

And then one day, Peter Daley grabbed me in the cafeteria. "Dude, why didn't you tell us?" he said.

"Tell you what?"

He dragged me to a table. Bob Hollins was there. And some other guys. Kirk came over too.

"Dude, you did it with some downtown chick. Kirk told us."

"I did *not* tell them," said Kirk.

"And it was the same night you totaled your car!" They all seemed to think this was the height of cool. Kirk rolled his eyes.

"And she was some punk chick!" said Peter. "Dude that is like . . . that is so not like you!"

"You could have done it with Cindy," said Bob. "You blew it. Twice."

"Why don't you shut up," said Kirk.

"I'm not saying it's bad," Peter said to me. "It's awesome. Was she hot?"

"I don't want to talk about it," I said.

"Obviously she was not hot," said Bob Hollins.

"Hey, I wouldn't be choosy," said Peter. "I just want to do it. Now that Max's done it, I'm the last one."

"I just hope she wasn't a total skank," said Bob Hollins.

"Hey asshole," Kirk said to Bob. "Why don't you try not being a complete idiot for once?"

"What are you blaming me for?" sneered Bob. "You're the one who knows all these freaks. You're the one who goes out with fat Becky What's-Her-Name."

Kirk hit Bob in the face with the Coke he was drinking. Then he exploded out of his seat, jumped over the table, and wrestled Bob Hollins to the floor.

Normally we might have let them go for a while. But at Evergreen you got massively busted for fighting. So we all jumped in and pulled them apart before anyone saw.

# 58 - - - - - - - - - - - -

My parents were right about one thing: not having a car was a serious punishment. I was back to riding the bus. It was February and raining every day, and there I stood, with my backpack and my stupid rain parka, waiting at the bus stop.

My mom was still pissed. She couldn't get over it somehow. It got so weird around the house, I couldn't even go into the TV room. Sometimes I wouldn't go home at all. I would ride the bus to Woodridge Mall. I'd walk around or get a coffee and write out editorial ideas in the food court.

One night, for variety, I took the bus across town to Lloyd Center Mall. I walked around and ended up on a bench watching the ice-skaters like I had done with Cindy.

That's when I saw Drea and Billy Hutchinson in the Cinnabon. That was a surprise. They were standing at the counter. Drea was ordering something. Why were they at Lloyd Center? How did they get there?

I slunk down so they wouldn't see me. I watched them. My sister was still having a miserable freshman year. Her grades were terrible. Her teachers said she was withdrawn. There had been a special meeting with my parents at Christmas. And now, with my accident, everyone had forgotten about her again.

And yet, there she was, with Billy Hutchinson, somehow managing to have a life. The weird part was that the Billy Hutchinson thing was supposedly over. Or had never got started. That's what Drea had told Mom and Dad. In fact, she had partially blamed it on me, for snooping too much.

Obviously, the Billy Hutchinson thing was very much alive. I watched them. He was a lot taller than her. She kept glancing up at him and biting her lip. I wanted to stay, but I was afraid they'd see me. So I got up and discreetly walked in the other direction. When I took a last peek, Billy was holding two hot chocolates while Drea cleaned off a table with a napkin.


"Since when do you smoke weed?" said Kirk.

"Since right now," I told him. We were standing on the street outside the Air Hockey Café. It was open mike poetry night. Monica and Becky were inside. Monica was signed up to read some poems.

Kirk handed me the joint he was smoking. I had never really smoked pot. I took some and had a minor coughing fit. I gave it back to Kirk. He took more. I took more.

We watched the reading through the window. Then Kirk did an imitation of one of the poets. We both started giggling about it, right in the street. It got kind of crazy. We started laughing really hard and giggling . . . we couldn't stop . . . it was strange but really fun and I could feel my brain kind of . . . going away from me . . . with the giggling and the stupid jokes we were making . . . I was going away from myself, separating from myself . . . but joining with Kirk in some way and feeling like . . . this deep, warm happiness in my chest that was incredible and eventually made me really crave some, like, something with sugar in it . . . so then we went down the street to the Handy-Mart where we bought

Doritos and Ho Hos and all this stuff . . . and we kept laughing and trying to pay for it but we couldn't find our money and then Kirk pulled his pocket inside out and all these pennies were rolling around and I laughed so hard I was literally afraid my guts would burst. . . .

We missed Monica's reading, and afterward she was pissed at us. Becky, fortunately, had some beer, and we drove around and listened to music. I felt so happy, so unbelievably happy but also these strange thoughts kept hitting me out of nowhere, like wondering what happened to my parents . . . when did they start hating me so much? . . . had they always hated me? . . . was everything I ever did just to make them stop hating me . . . ?

# 59 - - - - - - - - - - - - - -

The new *Owl* came out. I saw one of the stacks in the cafeteria and had the strange sensation of not recognizing it. I stopped and picked up a copy. It was different from the final version I thought we had okayed. It was most of the same stories, Lydia was in her usual spot, but everything else had been re-arranged.

I found Maria Sanchez at her locker. "Maria," I said, holding the paper. "What happened to the front page?"

"What do you mean?"

"It's all different."

She looked at me carefully. "No, it's not."

"I thought Jill St. John's thing was going to be in a big box at the bottom."

"Oh that," she said. "We had to change it. You were gone. You and Kirk had already left."

"Why did you—"

"It didn't fit. Kevin did something with the font. The computer version didn't fit. So we shuffled it around."

I looked at the paper. That made sense.

"We didn't change anything, Max. It's not like we did something behind your back."

"No, I know, I just—"

"If you want to be involved in everything that happens, you have to stay until it's done."

That night after school, I did hang around the *Owl*, but nothing was happening, so Kirk and Bryce and I went and shot baskets in the back parking lot. Then Bob Hollins and Dave Winchell came by and wanted to play. There was instant tension between Kirk and Bob, but nobody said anything.

Bryce left and we played two on two. I kind of arranged it so Kirk and Bob would be on the same team. But they were still getting pissed at each other. Eventually Bob Hollins said something I didn't hear, and Kirk threw the ball, and I had to grab him and walk him away into the parking lot.

- - -

Saturday night at Agenda, Kirk and Becky and Monica and I were hanging out. I was dancing with Monica when Danielle came in. The sight of her hit me hard. I kept dancing, but I kept myself hidden from her. I stayed lost in the crowd.

With all the excitement, I had not thought much about Danielle. I mean, I thought about what happened, but not like, what would I do if I saw her at Agenda.

I was at a loss. When the song ended Kirk and I retreated to our table.

"Danielle's here," I said.

"I know."

"What should I do?"

"Go talk to her?" said Kirk.

"I can't."

"Then don't."

Danielle was trying to talk to Brian Brain and another guy at one of the back tables. But they were not interested in talking to Danielle. You could see they didn't want her to sit with them. She did it anyway. About ten minutes later they got up and walked away, leaving Danielle sitting there by herself.

"Ouch," said Kirk.

"I know," I said.

"Maybe you'd better stay away from her."

Later, I went to Kirk's car with Monica. It was raining and cold, and we had to cover each other with our coats while we fooled around.

"Max?" she whispered as she pulled on my belt.

"Yeah?"

"Are we being bad?"

"Yeah, I guess so."

"I like being bad," she whispered. "Do you like being bad?"

"Could you not talk?"

"Don't you like to talk?"

"I just don't want to think about it."

# 60

"Max?" said Lydia. "Hel-lo? Anyone there?"

I woke up, dropping my feet off Mr. Owens' desk abruptly. It was lunchtime. We were in the *Owl* office.

"What?" I said.

"What do you think of my new column?"

"I think it's good."

"You didn't even read it."

"Yes I did. I think we should chop off the last paragraph."

"You always say that."

"No, but, it makes it more . . . "

She crossed her arms and stared at me.

"What?" I said.

We went to McDonald's. Lydia had a car now, so that was good. I was glad to be out of the *Owl*.

I got a Big Mac Value Meal. Lydia watched me eat. I ate my Big Mac and my fries and dipped some of my fries in her milkshake.

"So what's up with you?" said Lydia.

"Nothing."

"That car accident shook you up."

"No, it didn't."

"How's Cindy?"

"How would I know?"

She stared at me. I chewed my Big Mac. She slapped my hand away when I tried to dip a French fry in her milkshake. "Max," she said, with sudden seriousness.

"What?"

"I'm not going to embarrass myself by saying this more than once but I'm going to say it because I'll feel bad if I don't. . . ."

"What?"

"I just want to say . . . If you . . . If you need me. Or just someone. You know . . ."

"What?"

"I just want to say that besides being your annoying columnist I am also your friend."

"Jesus, why is everyone *my friend* lately? I got in a car accident. Big deal. Why am I everybody's favorite charity case all of a sudden?"

"I had a feeling you would say that. All right. Never mind."

"I'm getting kind of sick of this attitude everyone's copping—"

*"Forget it,"* she said again. "Never mind. I'm going. You can finish my milkshake if you want."

"I don't want your milkshake."

She got up. She walked out. I had to walk back to the *Owl* in the rain.


That night I worked late at the *Owl*. Maria Sanchez offered to give me a ride home, but I couldn't bear the thought of talking to her for the fifteen minutes it would take to get me home. So I waited for the bus. But I didn't really want to go home. When the downtown bus came, I ran across the street and got on that.

I went to Agenda. It was a Thursday night, so there weren't too many people. I got a smoothie from the juice bar and sat at a table and watched the kids coming in.

Then I felt a hand on my elbow. "Max," said a voice.

I turned. It was Eleanor.

"Eleanor! Wow! I can't believe it's you," I said. "When did you—" but I shut up. It was not cool to become too excited around Eleanor.

"I like to sneak into town now and then," she said, sitting beside me.

"It's so great to see you," I said. I smiled at her and sipped my smoothie through the straw.

We sat for a moment in silence. "How's school?" she said.

"It's almost over," I said.

"Have you learned anything?"

"Not recently. I've been going backward kind of recently."

"How so?"

"I don't know," I said. I sipped my smoothie again. Someone waved at Eleanor and she waved back. Then a little herd of young girls, Eleanor fans, came running across the dance floor to gush over her.

"Oh my god!"

"Eleanor!"

"Will you hang out with us sometime? Will you go shopping?"

Eleanor was polite but reserved. Eventually they left. But more people were seeing her. More people were going to come over.

"So how are you going backward?" she said.

"I tried to get back with my old girlfriend."

"How did that go?"

"Terrible."

"How come?"

"I'm not sure exactly," I said.

"Did you still have feelings for her?"

"Of course. I loved her. I loved her more than anything."

The DJ interrupted everything with an announcement. Someone's lights were on in the parking lot.

"Well that's sad then," said Eleanor.

I stirred my smoothie. "Have you ever been in love?"

"Sure. But probably different from you. I don't really . . . " She didn't finish the sentence.

I said, "The thing I don't understand is you love someone and you want everything to be right for them, you want them to be totally happy. But just by loving them you end up hurting them. Because something always happens."

Eleanor nodded. "But that's the fun of it. Of course something happens. And you end up in tears or jumping off a bridge or having screaming fights in the middle of some party." She smiled to herself at the thought of it. "Some people like that stuff."

"Why?"

She shrugged. "It makes them feel alive."

"I don't need screaming fights to make me feel alive."

"Are you sure? Maybe that's why you went back with her."

I frowned at her. I sucked down the rest of my smoothie. A girl shrieked from across the room, "Eleanor! Is that you!?" A little punk girl in a pink dress came running toward us. Soon Eleanor was surrounded by friends.

# 61

"Hi Max."

"Hi Mr. Owens."

"Come in, sit down," he said.

I entered his office and shut the door. I sat down across from his desk. He smiled at me. I smiled back.

"How are you doing?" he asked.

"I'm all right. What's up?"

"Nothing really. I just wanted to touch base, see how things are going."

"Things are going okay," I said. "Everything is . . . back to normal I guess. I'm all healed up."

He watched me. "How's the new editorial going."

"It sucks. All my editorials suck."

"Editorials are hard. It's hard for a student to try to . . . *instruct* the other students."

"You'd think I'd be good at it."

"Why do you say that?"

"I don't know," I said. I shifted in my seat. "No reason."

He smiled.

I smiled.

"So how's your sister?" he said.

"My sister?"

"Andrea Caldwell? I assume she's your sister."

"Yeah. Drea. We call her Drea."

"I just took over Mrs. Bowman's freshman English class. Since she's pregnant. So I have Andrea now. She seems like a nice girl."

"She is. She's nice."

"How about your parents? How are they?"

"They're fine."

"College applications must all be out. So you're no doubt waiting for that."

"Yeah." I nodded. "Waiting to hear."

"It must be hard to keep focused."

"Not that hard," I said.

He sat there watching me. I avoided looking at him. I looked at the top of my right shoe. I thought, *That's the top of my right shoe.*

"All right," said Mr. Owens. "I guess that's all. Glad to see you're fully recovered."

"Yeah, I'm pretty much back to normal."

"If there's anything you ever need . . . "

I nodded. "Yeah, sure. Thanks."

The new *Owl* came out. It was one of our worst issues. Even with Lydia's column, "What Guys Really Want," on the front page. It sat in stacks for two days.

We had an *Owl* meeting. But people weren't focused. There was a general restlessness. We talked about "Voices." Kirk's new question was: "High school or prison, which gives a more practical education?" This was supposed to be funny, but when we asked people, they thought we were serious. So then we tried: "Where will you be ten years from now?" But the answers were boring. So I suggested: "What event in your life has made you question the existence of God?"

Everyone stared at me.

"What?" I said. "It's a joke. Jeez, you guys."

After the meeting I thought maybe Lydia and I could hang out, but when I sat down next to her she wouldn't look at me. She immediately began packing up her stuff.

"What are you doing now?" I asked her.

"I have to go."

"Where?"

"Home."

I watched her put her notebook in her backpack.

"What? Are you mad at me now?" I said.

"No."

"Why are you being weird?"

"I'm not being weird."

The next day I saw Cindy in the hall. She actually looked at me and didn't turn away. It was strange the way she did it. But I was so confused now. I had no idea what it meant.

And then after school I was walking past the back parking lot and I saw two guys go running down the hill toward the baseball diamond. By the way they were running, I knew something important was happening. I ran too. I got to the edge of the hill. Bob Hollins and Kirk were fighting at the bottom. A group of guys were gathered around.

I ran down the hill. It was a serious fight. Kirk's shirt was ripped half off his body. Bob Hollins's mouth was dripping blood. Everyone looked up as I came down the hill. They expected me to take charge, to break it up and restore order.

But I didn't. I attacked Bob Hollins. He was so surprised he didn't even defend himself. I threw myself at him and started punching him in the head.

Everyone jumped in. Someone grabbed me from behind. Everyone was pushing and pulling and trying to break it up. In the chaos, another kid got knocked into me. The back of his head hit me right in the face. Right in the nose.

It was the same male nurse at the entrance to the ER, and the same doctor. He didn't joke this time. The nurses didn't either. My dad stood behind him while he examined my nose. His fingers felt cold and creepy in his latex gloves.

Another nurse brought in the X-rays. They put them up on the lighted box. The doctor talked to my dad. I didn't really listen. I knew it wasn't broken. It had bled a lot but it didn't hurt like the other time.

"All right, young man," said the doctor, gesturing for me to get off the examining table.

I slid off it. I put on my coat.

My dad drove me home. We didn't talk. Fighting at Evergreen was a mandatory three-day suspension. Fortunately for me, people lied and told Mr. Brown that I was trying to break it up. So they made an exception. Kirk and Bob Hollins were both suspended for three days. I only got one.

# 62

It was almost midnight when we got home. My poor mother. I couldn't face her. I got out of my dad's Camry and tried to sneak through the house and up the stairs to my room.

She was waiting for me though. "Max, you come down here this second," she said.

I stopped at the top of the stairs.

"Max Caldwell, you come down here!"

I turned. I looked at her. I had never seen her so angry.

I came slowly down the stairs. I was a mess. My shirt was bloody, my pants were covered with mud and grass stains, my hair was stuck to my forehead.

"What do you have to say for yourself?" she said.

I stared at the wall behind her.

"Say something young man!"

"I'm a National Merit Scholar," I said, without emotion. "I was captain of the debate team. I'm a straight-A student and the editor of the school paper. That's what I am. What more could you possibly want?"

I turned and went back up the stairs.


I hadn't snuck out of my room since I was twelve years old. It came back to me though: quietly open the window, crawl out, carefully slide down the roof about eight feet to the rain gutter. Then move sideways to where the back fence was. Lower myself to the top fence post, balance, and then jump to the grass. I barely made a sound.

And then I felt the incredible joy of having the whole night to myself, the whole world. I had thought there was a lot of freedom being a good student, being trusted, being given special privileges, but that was nothing compared to the freedom I felt now. Once people gave up on you, once people wrote you off, now *that* was freedom.

I started walking. For the first mile I thought I was going to Kirk's. But his house was too far away. So I changed my course and started walking toward my old middle school.

Then I changed it again because I was near Lydia's house. It was too late to visit, but it gave me a direction.

I found Lydia's street. I had never been inside her house, but I had dropped her off. So I knew which one it was. I approached it now. It was a pretty typical house for that neighborhood, two-story, with a daylight basement. I saw that there was someone awake in one of the basement rooms. I could see the light on the grass by the side of the house. I walked around to that side. I crept along the side of the house. I approached the window and looked in.

It was Lydia. In her room. She was in her bathrobe. She was sitting at her computer.

I tapped on the window.

- - - - - - - - - - - - - **63**

"Shhh, Max, be quiet . . . " said Lydia, as she pulled me through the window.

The metal frame dug into my hands and my stomach as I wiggled over it. I finally rolled forward and landed upside down on the floor of her bedroom.

"Shhhh . . . " she said as she helped me up. Then she saw the blood on the front of my shirt. "Oh no! What—?"

"Don't worry," I said. "It's old."

She led me away from the window. She brushed at my

shoulders, cleaning me off as best she could. "God, look at you. You look awful. What are you doing here?"

"Just . . . walking."

"I hope my mother didn't hear you." She went to her door and crept down the hall to see if I'd woken anyone up.

She came back. She quietly shut the door. I was still standing in the middle of the room.

"Sit," she said. She motioned me to her bed. I sat down on it.

She sat beside me. "Well. This is an interesting surprise."

"I know."

"Just out for a walk at . . . one-thirty in the morning?" she asked.

"Hey, you're awake too."

"I know. I couldn't sleep."

I looked around her room. "I won't stay. I just needed to get out of the house."

"It's all right," she said. "Everyone's asleep."

We sat there.

"Also, I uh . . ." I said, lowering my head, "I kind of wanted to apologize."

"Don't. Max. Like you need to say anything."

"Still . . ."

"Do you want something to eat?" she said, cheerfully. "We have Pop-Tarts."

"No thanks."

We sat there. It was awkward but it was okay. I felt like I could breathe again. I was very glad I had come.

"What are you working on?" I asked finally, looking at her computer screen.

"Just . . . reading some girl in Wisconsin's diary. Looking for column ideas."

"That's where you get your ideas?" I asked.

"Yeah, sometimes."

"Everybody loves your column," I said. "I guess you hear that a lot."

"Not from you," she said.

I looked around the room some more. I thought about all the times I had talked to Lydia on the phone. This was where she was when we talked.

"Do your parents know you're gone?" she said.

"No," I said. There was a lot to look at in Lydia's room. There were pictures and articles and posters stuck on the walls. There was a picture of Nathan Reimer from the paper. It was thumb-tacked to a bulletin board over her computer.

"I guess I'd better go," I said.

"You don't have to. Really. Do you want to take off your coat?"

I took it off. She put it over a chair. Then she unbuttoned my dirty shirt and helped me take that off. Then she went into her laundry room to find me something clean to wear. She came back with one of her dad's sweatshirts. I put it on. It was too big, and we kind of laughed about it, and then somehow we ended up hugging each other.

It was weird. I mean, it wasn't a sexual thing. We didn't kiss or anything. We just sort of came together. Like magnets. And once I felt her warmth, and her arms around me, I wasn't going to let go. I couldn't.

We eventually lay back on the bed. It was exactly what I needed: to hold someone and close my eyes and feel safe for a minute. Then I started to cry. Which was embarrassing. But I let myself. I had to. And the more I cried, the more she held me. And the more I cried.

# Epilogue

So yeah, that's pretty much the story. How I went from being one of those Mr. Perfect, straight-A types to . . . well . . . whatever I am now. Probably pretty much the same, though it doesn't always feel that way. I still have the vague feeling that something profound happened during that year. I don't know what exactly, but at some point, I seemed to cross a bridge, and from that moment on some other version of Max was back behind me, irretrievable, a better version, or at least a less complicated one.

But I'm making it sound more dramatic than it is. Everything worked out. I finished senior year without further incident. I never even served my one-day suspension. In April I got into several excellent colleges and am presently a sophomore at Yale. I am doing okay, though I don't get the grades I used to. It's good though. I like college. I'm the type for it.

Also, in case anyone is wondering, Lydia and I did not

end up together. We remained close friends, but something about that night—it was too intense, it took a week before I could look her in the eye again. I know that's not showing much gratitude on my part. But whatever. She understood. She's kind of amazing that way. It's probably why she's such a good writer.

I didn't date anyone seriously after that. Cindy was and remained my one great high school love. I never even talked to Danielle again. Or Monica. But that happened with Agenda people. They would blow through your life and then vanish into thin air.

Eleanor, on the other hand, I suspect I will see again. I don't know why I think that but I do.


What else? Lydia is a senior and is currently editor of the *Owl*. She no longer writes a column but is instead stuck writing editorials. Mr. Owens is still there advising. Mr. Owens wrote me a great college recommendation, by the way. It was he who really got me in here.

Jill St. John went to Reed. I see her when I'm back in Portland. She always invites me over for herbal tea. She's still beautiful and brilliant and very opinionated. She has a new boyfriend, another handsome activist guy, who works at a bakery.

Kirk is at the University of Oregon. He's no longer writing about music, he's playing it. He sent me a tape of his new band, The Scepters. They play noisy garage rock.

I don't know where Becky Cetera is. Maria Sanchez supposedly went to Smith, but I haven't heard from her. Cindy is a freshman and in a sorority at the University of Oregon. She's probably having a great time. I hope so.

Lydia is the only one I really stay in touch with. My first year away we didn't communicate much, but once she took over the *Owl*, we started e-mailing regularly. It started with her asking questions, like: How do you make articles about football interesting? How do you cover student government without falling asleep? But of course, these are the unanswerable questions that have tormented mankind throughout history.

I like hearing from her, and I have to say, the *Owl* looks pretty good with her in charge. She sends me copies of it. It's funny, because now that she has to write the editorials she's stuck in the same trap I was. As editor you have to be responsible and authoritative. And therefore, you suck!

It cracks me up. I tease her about it. Her paper's good, but my paper was better. I had her.

## Acknowledgments:

Thanks: Regina Hayes and Catherine Frank, Charlotte Sheedy and Carolyn Kim, Sally Cohen, Victoria Wells Arms, Amanda Ayers, Giulia Melucci, Cary Hoffman, Jackie Phelan, Drew, Heidi, Penny, Paula, James, Little James, Misha, Nick Chin, John Fahs, Craig Lesley, Don Waters and John DeWitt and all the good people at VERSUS PRESS, Jonathan Nicholas, Christina Kelly and Molly Rosen, everyone at Powell's, Gabe and Jen, everyone at Tribeca, Doug Rushkoff and the HL Group, Ben Schrank, Janice Eidus, Richard Martin, Cat Tyc, Craig Foltz, Gary Hustwit, and Linda Ann Edwards.